F

a novel by Brittney Kristina

Edited Edition

Printed in the United States of America

First Printing, 2016

ISBN 1537043609

Createspace Independent Publishing
www.createspace.com

Hot Tree Editing

Cover Design by Najla Qamber

"Great read. Great price. Give this young author a chance to impress you."

"Love the creativity in this book!"

"Greatly enjoyed it!"

"This story is fantastic!"

"Such an interesting way to tell a story, and I was definitely entertained from beginning to end."

"Good writing is supposed to evoke sensation in the reader: Not the fact that it is raining, but the feeling of being rained upon."

~ E.L. Doctorow

I would like to thank my several family members and friends who have helped make this novel possible. I couldn't choose just one person to appreciate! You all know who you are.

And to everyone else:
Welcome to my mind.

Contents

one

"Hello, Skylar."

I glance up to see a woman stroll into the office. She's frail, a tight pink dress fitting loose against her skin. Her hands are bony as she clutches some papers, pressing them firmly against her chest as if she cannot let them fall from her grasp. She smiles brightly, and the whiteness of her teeth seems to sting my solemn stare, but then her lips carefully lower and her expression is more comforting. Abruptly, she rips her attention from me and stares forward.

"How are you today?" It seems as though she says it to the air.

I watch as she walks quickly to the brown desk before me, sliding the papers into yellow folders. Her fingers are gentle, her meticulous ways somewhat mesmerizing. Her face is plain but her gaze is wild, as if she is paying such close attention to the papers that she somehow forgets of my presence.

She stops moving then, turning to me with a sudden worried expression. Her eyes are green, like emeralds. I'm surprised I've just now noticed this. I stiffen; he had green eyes, too.

"I'm sorry," she mumbles, a smile slowly spreading onto her face again, soft and sincere. "I'm afraid I've been incredibly busy today. My mind is all over the place." She pushes a strand of red hair behind her left ear, fetching a clipboard and a pencil before sitting on the love seat across from me. Her body is so thin she nearly disappears into the thick leather. I grin at that.

"Anyway," she continues, "I suppose I didn't directly introduce myself. My name is Mrs. Carter, but you may call me Susan if you'd like. I'll be your counselor while you're here."

"Don't you have a PhD?" I ask her flatly.

"Excuse me?"

"To be a counselor, you need a PhD," I tell her with cold eyes. "Shouldn't I call you *Dr.* Carter?"

She offers me a sour smile. "Well, yes, I'm technically a doctor. But I've concluded that 'Mrs.' sounds more welcoming than 'Dr.' Do you agree?"

I shrug, wrapping my arms around myself and slouching over, staring to the floor.

"Are you all right? Do you need a blanket?"

I don't reply.

Mrs. Carter lets out a deep breath. "Would you like to tell me about yourself?" She says this slowly, as if her words could break my delicate body.

I glance up at her, gritting my teeth. *Why am I here? What is the point of this?*

"Skylar is certainly a lovely name. I've always—"

"No."

She looks at me funny; her nose wrinkled like she's just smelled an odd odor of some sort. I sniff the cold air but smell nothing but coffee. However, that isn't exactly a new smell; this entire place reeks of it.

"No, what, sweetie?"

"I don't want to talk about myself," I reply flatly, then turn my attention to a nearby wall. All of the walls in here are painted a light brown color, sort of like a darkened sand. I think of sand, and then of the beach. I wish I were at the beach instead. I close my eyes, imagining the blue waters, the sunlight warm on my skin. I can taste the salt in the air. But I open my eyes and see the counselor again, and I frown.

"Then what would you like to talk about?" Mrs. Carter wonders quietly, almost as if she is speaking to herself.

I sigh. "Nothing."

"All right," she replies, so quickly it nearly scares me. Then she smiles again. "Take your time, Skylar. I don't want you to rush into anything, because you've already been through a lot. It's perfectly understandable." She looks down and scribbles something on a paper clipped to her clipboard.

"So I don't have to talk?"

She looks up. "If you're not ready, we don't have to talk."

So we sit in silence, and I imagine the beach.

. . . .

I stare up at the ceiling, counting the squares, or tiles, or whatever they are. It's so boring in here, definitely more boring than back home. Every two hours a nurse will come in to check on me or bring me a meal, not that I'll eat it, or a doctor will randomly enter, and run a few tests. But besides that—as well as going to Mrs. Carter's office, obviously—I sit in here, a room full of white with giant glass windows on the wall in front of me. Every now and then someone will walk by those windows, usually in a hurry, and I try to wonder where they are headed to, or coming from. I try to think of what their lives are like, and most of the time I figure they are exciting, at least more so than mine. I doubt any of them are as boring as mine.

I wasn't always this way, sitting in a room, alone, counting the squares on the ceiling. I used to be a normal teenager. I used to have friends, and I used to go to school every day and come home every night to television. I was nice, I think, and fairly funny. But now I'm some psycho in a mental facility.

I close my eyes and think back to just three months ago. I was sitting in class, geometry, solving some problems about circles or something. I glanced up for an unknown reason when I saw Zack Corley—*the* Zack Corley—looking straight at me. My eyes grew so wide I swear they nearly popped from the sockets. I pressed my lips into a tight line, so tight they grew numb. He grinned at me and turned away.

That was the happiest moment of my life then, because trust me, Zack Corley isn't your average high school sophomore. He's handsome, with blond hair and striking blue eyes, and his teeth are whiter than this room I sit in now. Zack is the captain of the soccer team, with a body better than a Ken doll, and skin so tan you'd think he lived in California, not New York City. He's literally every girl's dream. I didn't know a single living soul who didn't wish they could kiss him, marry him, or *be* him. And he smiled at *me*, the sort of quiet book-nerd with liquid blue eyes and skin as pale as a vampire standing amongst a misty forest. Nobody noticed me except for the few friends or acquaintances I had, never mind *Zack Corley*.

As soon as the bell rang, Zack walked by me quickly, glancing at me sharply up and down. He pressed a hand through his perfect locks, sending me a quick smile before continuing out the door. I blushed as I watched him go, my body frozen in place. I hoped nobody noticed.

Later that day, I of course ran straight to Andria once I saw her. "Guess what!" I squealed, just like any normal girl would if Zack Corley smiled at them.

"Oh my gosh, what?" Andria replied, all jittery and excited already. I figured she already knew what I was going to say; her smile crazed and her brown eyes turning milky, her black hair messy, her bangs tangled across her forehead. She'd acquired those bangs the previous summer, and she liked them more than chocolate, so of course, I didn't tell her that she actually looked five with them, especially with the freckles painted across her nose.

"Zack," I said, breathless, "*smiled* at me."

"You're kidding."

"No! I swear he did!"

"Oh my gosh, you're not kidding!"

And we jumped up and down and cheered together until the warning bell rang and we had to head to class, our hearts still racing.

I open my eyes, sitting up in my bed and gazing forward to the windows. That was only three months ago, a few weeks after Matt and I broke up, and I thought I was moving on—or in other words, when life was normal and fun, and everything was a game, a joke. Now, my mind is at war.

My eyes cloud with tears as I remember Zack. Does he even notice my absence? I doubt it. He never noticed me again after that one smile, and I thought it was so important. The best thing that could've ever happened to me. But now it's all so pointless. After that night, that world... everything is so pointless to me.

. . . .

"So, Skylar, are you feeling any better? Are you ready to talk?"

It is the next day. I've been here three days now.

I adjust myself in the love seat, pulling my T-shirt down over my knees. It's way too big for me, but I don't really mind it.

"It's okay if you're not ready, Skylar."

I shake my head. "I just have a lot on my mind, I guess." I swallow. "If I start speaking, I'll end up saying all of it. I might go crazy again."

Mrs. Carter smiles. "We're all a little bit crazy, huh? We can't help it at times."

"But I'm a psycho."

"Why do you believe that?" she asks, her head falling to one side and her eyebrows furrowing.

"I just...." I trail off, biting my bottom lip. "What happened that night... it's messing with my head."

"Well, of course it is," Mrs. Carter answers calmly. "Dreams tend to do that sometimes."

I stare at her hard. "But it wasn't a dream."

Her eyes widen. "Really?"

"Yes. I'm sure of it."

She crosses her ankles and sits up straighter, her eyes cold, studying me. Analyzing my every breath. "Now, Skylar," she says steadily. "Would you mind telling me what happened to you... that night?"

"I don't know," I murmur quickly. I don't really hear the question; it goes right over my head. I start to imagine the silence of that world, the chaos, the madness, and I stiffen, quickly deciding to think about something else. I focus on Zack, but his face fades. I try to think of anybody else I know, like Andria and Matt and Mom and

Dad, but all of their faces fade as well. "It's a lot to say," I whisper to myself. "It's complicated."

"That's perfectly fine," she replies with a grin, her expression softening.

I turn my eyes to the floor.

"Are you okay?"

"Yes," I murmur. "I just haven't exactly thought about what happened since, well, it happened."

"Really? And why is that?"

"I'm afraid," I admit. I mainly say this to myself, and the words feel bizarre on my tongue. I lick my lips, a knot suddenly caught in my throat.

"Afraid," Mrs. Carter repeats quietly. "That's an interesting adjective to use. What are you afraid of?"

"Remembering."

Mrs. Carter doesn't reply immediately. Instead, she writes something down on her paper again. "And why is remembering so frightening?" she asks at last, her voice slicing through the silence.

"It's a lot to say."

She looks up then, eyeing me curiously. "Would you be open to sharing, Skylar?"

I swallow. Perhaps it would be nice to let it out. But then again, I'm not sure if I'm comfortable saying it. I'm barely comfortable just casually talking now.

"Skylar?"

I look at her, noticing the deep interest within her eyes. And suddenly, to my very surprise, the ensnared words slip from my tongue with such simplicity, sliding down my lips and pouring gently out of my mouth like a mellow stream.

two

I immediately figured that something was different that morning. It wasn't because my head ached, and it wasn't because my heart raced. It wasn't because goose bumps spread over every inch of my skin, and it *definitely* wasn't because the air was cold and thick with a bitter smell.

It was because of the silence.

My eyes opened wide and I gazed about my bedroom. Everything appeared normal; the clothes were where I had last left them the night before, and so were the pillows and books. But I knew something was wrong. The silence was biting at my ears, coating my body like a second skin. There was that ring in my ear, that buzz— the one you only have when there's so much quiet that your mind has to make up its own noise to listen to.

I sat up in bed, scratching my head and rubbing my eyes. My brain was still half asleep and my sight was hazy. I had this feeling, a not-so-good feeling filling up my stomach with an uncomfortable welcoming, filling my mouth with a sour taste.

I carefully slid from my comforters and made my way to my bedroom window, the carpet strange between my toes. As I neared the window, I grew all the more anxious. My palms were clammy and my knees trembled. Why was I so afraid? Perhaps because I had never endured this kind of silence before. No one had. No one who had lived in New York City their entire life, at least. No one like me.

The fog glazed over the glass panes. I smeared it away with a shaky hand, and the first thing I saw was the tall business property across from our apartment building, and the moss that covered it like a dress. *Moss. Has it always been there?* I figured it had and I had only now noticed the thick, green plant. The vines draped across the building, along with every other one in sight, as though the city had been abandoned for years. The thought made my stomach plummet.

I then looked down to the streets, where I saw nothing. *Literally* nothing. Not one living soul, not even the everyday pigeons pecking at bread crumbs on the sidewalk or dogs shuffling through trash cans. There were a few cars parked on the sides of the roads, and plastic bags rolling through the wind, yet there was absolutely nothing otherwise.

I slowly stepped back, a million thoughts and questions rushing through my mind all at once. Where was everybody? Why had they fled the streets? In New York City, something like that wasn't common, *ever*. I pressed my quivering palms to my forehead, pushing my curly red hair from my eyes. I couldn't process what was happening. My skin grew warm and clammy, and my bottom lip trembled as I tried to take everything in.

It was a normal Saturday, or at least it was supposed to be. I was going to sleep in, eat waffles or something, and then probably just go to the mall and people watch. But now everyone was gone and there was moss on the buildings.

I tried to listen for the sound of the coffee pot, but I couldn't find it. Mom normally woke up early and turned it on, waiting for it to brew while watching the news. I didn't hear the TV, either. Only that buzz. But I guessed Mom was still asleep. Perhaps she was running late. I'd just go to her, wake her up, and tell her what I saw. Yes, of course. She'd know what to do because she's wise. She's an adult.

I'm only sixteen. I'm not supposed to figure this kind of stuff out for myself. I'm still a child. Or at least that's what Mom tells me on the days that she cares, or when I try to do something rebellious—which isn't exactly too often but often enough to remember you're a helpless baby in the house.

I walked from my room to see more emptiness in our small, two-bedroom apartment. And as I suspected, neither the news, nor any TV, nor the coffee pot was on. I swallowed loudly.

It's eight thirty in the morning. Mom wouldn't sleep in this late, would she?

I made my way past the kitchen and living room, which were basically combined into one small space, to Mom's bedroom. That same nervousness crept over me from when I walked to the window. I had a feeling she wouldn't be there, but then again, it was just a feeling.

"Mom?" I called before I opened the door, my fingers tight on the doorknob. I don't know why I spoke before walking in, but perhaps it was because I wanted to hear the sound of her voice. I didn't want to hear the silence anymore.

She didn't reply. I swallowed, my throat constricted and dry. "Mom." I squeaked it that time, my body so shaky I could hardly see straight. And when she didn't answer again, I cautiously opened the door.

She wasn't in the room. I'll admit that I wasn't exactly surprised, but I was still incredibly freaked out.

"Mom?" I continued to call even when I knew she wasn't there, tossing pillows and blankets while I did. I checked under the bed and even in her dresser, but she was gone. Just like the rest of New York City as it seemed. I was alone.

I knew it couldn't be possible. I ran to the nearest window and looked out once again to see those same vacant streets that sent a shiver through my spine once before. Blinking back the tears, I gulped so hard my neck started to ache, my jaw clenched. I couldn't believe it. Was I really alone? It seemed that way.

I made my way back to my room slowly, my eyes tired and wet and a sick feeling spreading throughout my skin, making me weak. I hadn't ever felt that way before... not since the day Dad left us, at least. The familiar feeling suffocated me—that feeling of being alone. Abandoned. Forsaken.

I picked up my phone and called Andria, no matter our current situation. No answer. I called my ex-boyfriend, Matt, even. No answer. I called a few friends from my classes. No answers. Then I called my Dad. I'm not even sure the number still worked; he never answered on a good day. As predicted, he didn't answer any of the eleven calls.

I started laughing. It was a creepy laugh, almost evil. I'm not sure why I laughed, but then again I wasn't really sure about anything at the moment.

"This is just a dream," I told myself, nodding. "Yeah, it's just a stupid nightmare." But it seemed so real. I could feel the thick air around me, and I could breathe it in. But I knew such a happening as this couldn't be scientifically possible. Everyone in New York City besides me couldn't just *disappear*. Right?

I decided to take a shower, rinse away the worries. Before I did though, I stared at my somber expression in the mirror. My pale eyes were drained, and my orange-red hair was wild and matted to my head in odd places. I still had a morning face, my nose overly big, and my lips too thin. I was short, so I could only see to my shoulders in the bathroom mirror. Who knows why Mom placed it so high on the wall. I'm about five-foot-three. I got that from my mom, because she's five-foot-four. Dad was tall, nearly six-foot.

I'm sorry, I'm getting off topic.

Anyway, I stood beneath the warm water, letting my thoughts escape and roam freely among my mind. I was pretty certain it was a dream. Yeah, I was okay.

After the shower, I crept into bed without drying my hair. I wanted to get rid of this happening, this nightmare, as quickly as possible. I sat there, starving, wondering when I'd wake up. I closed my eyes, listening to the buzz, the ring. But no matter how loud it was, it still did not overthrow the piercing screams of the silence.

three

"I think that is enough for today," I say, stretching up, popping my back.

"Oh?" Mrs. Carter says, interest clouding her eyes.

I nod.

"Why?"

"I may say too much." I press a strand of hair behind my right ear, smacking my lips. "I do that sometimes."

"Well, that's fine. That's fine," she tells me, a smile appearing. "Next time we can talk more about what happened, okay?"

I look to the floor.

"Well," she continues, "that was certainly an interesting story."

My eyes dart up to her quickly, waiting for her to add something. When she doesn't, I say, "Oh, that wasn't all of it."

"It wasn't?" She appears oddly surprised.

I grin.

"Oh, well my bad. I thought wrong, I suppose."

"That's why I quit talking," I mumble. "There's too much to say."

"There's never too much to say," she laughs. Suddenly, her face hardens, her expression turning more serious. "Now Skylar, I must ask… do you still feel lonely since your dad left?"

"What?"

"I'm sorry, let me rephrase that. When your dad left, you said you felt lonely, abandoned. Do you still feel that way when you think of him?"

I don't answer.

"Well, that may be a cause of this first experience in your dream. The silence, the emptiness could be a relation to you and your father. You feel silenced by him, and alone, abandoned. And I believe that—"

"But it wasn't a dream!"

She stares at me, taken aback by my interruption. "Skylar, I just—"

"You weren't there," I grunt. "You're not allowed to tell me it was all for nothing, and that it was all made-up stuff based off my own loneliness."

"Skylar." She says my name slowly, stretching out the syllables. Her face seems sincere yet confused, as though she doesn't know what to say. "I'm sorry if that's how my words came across. I didn't mean to make them sound that way."

I frown, turning away.

"I understand you probably went through a very rough time that night and—"

"Until I finish telling you what happened," I say abruptly, "you cannot make assumptions."

"Okay, but—"

"No," I spat. "No more talking. I want to stop talking." I close my eyes quickly before she replies, and I think about the beach again.

. . . .

"Um, heck no," Andria growled beneath her breath. "Yellow does *not* look good on you."

"Ouch," I replied with a sly laugh. "Okay then." I turned around and headed back to the dressing room.

"No, Sky," Andria said, a little less negativity biting her tone. She said it as if she were sighing. "I didn't mean it like *that*. You know how I get when I shop." She laughed. "You look pretty in *everything*." I heard a smile in her voice.

"Too late for compliments," I laughed. "I'm going to go and cry now. Can you unzip me?"

"Shut up," she said as she delicately unzipped the bright yellow dress. It fell quickly, and I grasped it before I flashed everyone else in the store. "Good catch," she stated flatly. "Now go try on the green one."

"Aren't you going to try any on?" I wondered, walking into my dressing room and shutting the door. I slipped the itchy yellow dress off and grabbed the green one. I'd had my eye on it ever since we stepped foot into the boutique. I had a feeling it was the one.

"Not until you find one."

"We'll be here *forever*, then," I murmured.

"I'm sure the green one will look great." I thought so, too. "Come on, are you dressed yet?"

"Don't rush me."

"I'm not!"

"I've literally been in here for, like, twenty seconds."

"That's a lot of time."

"Ha-ha."

"Hurry up!"

I opened the door. "Zip me up." I turned around and felt her cold hands on my back as she handled the zipper. I sucked in my breath as the zipper flew up; I hadn't realized how tight it was. I wheezed.

"Oh my *gosh*," Andria cried.

"What?"

"Turn around." I did. She gasped, her eyes wide with amazement, her smile ear-to-ear. "It's *perfect*!"

"Nothing's perfect," I managed to squeak out. "It's so tight."

"Look in the mirror already!"

I turned to stare at my pale self in the mirror. The green certainly made my nearly-clear blue eyes pop, and my skin didn't seem as pale. The dress was strapless, the top half slick and soft with the bottom half covered in ruffles and bits of gold, like twinkling jewels. Even as much as I couldn't breathe, it was certainly beautiful. And although it was tight, it fit my small shape rather well.

"It's *breathtaking*," I joked.

Andria giggled. "*Literally*. I have a good eye. I'm glad I picked that one out. I'm good, aren't I? Don't I have a good eye?"

I glanced at her. "This is the only one you *didn't* pick out."

"Whatever." She rolled her eyes.

I turned to look at myself in the mirror again. It was strange wearing a dress that I actually felt good in. I've only worn a dress out once before, when we went to church on Easter when I was, like, seven. We haven't been back to church since.

"Andria, I don't even like dresses," I whispered.

"Well, start liking them because you're buying it."

"It's too much. And when would I ever wear it?"

"To homecoming, *duh*."

"Well, *yeah*. But what about after homecoming?"

"Uh, I don't know."

"Exactly."

"Skylar," Andria sighed. "You're getting it."

"But—"

"No buts. Now come on, let's go find one for me."

. . . .

The nurse, Amelia, walks into my room. It frightens me and I jump.

"Oh, dear," she says. "I didn't mean to scare you, honey."

I press my lips into a line and run a hand through my hair. It's so tangled and wild my fingers don't manage to continue all the way, and I end up getting them stuck in my curls.

Amelia is a very round, middle-aged woman with short brown hair tied back into a tight bun, and a thin nose. She smiles, her cheeks flushed as always. She reminds me of one of those huge teddy bears. I almost want to hug her; maybe her warmth would make me feel alive.

"Lunch," she says, overly cheerful as she raises a tray with a PB&J sandwich, an apple, chocolate pudding, and a glass of apple juice.

"I'm not hungry," I snap.

Her smile fades, yet she still appears happy. "Oh, honey. Please eat just once, at least."

"You can give me the tray, but I won't touch it."

She frowns. It unsettles me. "Do you want to lose more weight? I doubt you do, honey. You're as thin as a twig."

"Fine by me. I'm not trying to impress anyone, you know."

Amelia sighs, setting down the tray and sitting at the edge of my bed. I sit up straighter, uncomfortable. "Please," she begs. "Eat. You haven't eaten in three days."

"I don't care."

"Skylar, honey, listen. If you don't eat, you won't get any better."

I meet her soft eyes. My body stiffens. "Maybe I don't want to get better."

She bites her bottom lip. "Should I get the doctor?"

I shrug. "If you want." My eyes flick away to the floor.

"Skylar," she says harshly. "Do you want to die?"

My stare turns back to her, my eyebrows furrowed, and my body heated up. "You're not my freaking counselor," I spit out.

"No, but I am your nurse." She says this softly, as if she's trying to calm me with words.

"Go away!" I scream.

She blinks. "Skylar—"

"Get out! Just get out!" My face feels hot as I grit my teeth and lean forward. "Get *out!*"

"I will not get out until you eat that food." Her stare is firm.

"Fine." I pick up the tray, setting it on my lap. I look at the pudding, my eyes glassy, my brain dead. I can feel Amelia watching patiently, so I pick up the sandwich, raise it to my mouth. Then I throw it at Amelia and it hits her right in the face. She gasps, peanut butter and jelly covering her blue slacks.

"*Skylar!*"

"I said *get out!*"

She stands, no more happiness within her eyes. I've never seen a person so angry at me before. However, in a way, I'll admit it amuses me.

"Skylar," she whispers almost to herself, as if she's afraid, doesn't know what to do with me. I don't doubt her being scared of me now. I'm awful. I'm a psycho. I'm a *monster*.

I lift the tray, tears running down my face. She raises her hands in defense.

I want to stop myself. What the heck am I doing? I try to resist, but it's too late. I throw the tray at her, food flying, the cup falling and bouncing off the floor. The tray hits her directly in the forehead and she falls to the ground.

I look at her limp body. "What the heck is wrong with me?" I cry out. My vision is hazy, my frantic eyes not willing to focus on any specific thing. "Help!" I begin to scream to the air. "Somebody, *please* help!"

four

"Will she be okay?"

"Well—"

"Please, Doctor. She *has* to be okay." I shake my head. "She didn't deserve that."

Dr. Richards looks at me with sad eyes as he tightens the straps on my wrist. They hurt, and I'm afraid I may lose circulation. "I know," he replies coldly, looking down again.

"I'm sorry," I mumble.

He nods. "It's okay, Sky. But we'll just have to restrain you from now on." He looks up at me from the straps and steps back, crossing his arms. He's a very attractive man, probably forty-something. He has nice brown hair and warm brown eyes, large muscles popping from his dress shirt. He probably hooks up with all the nurses. But then I think of Amelia and feel sad. Probably not *all* of them.

"I understand."

He lets out a sigh. "Why did you do what you did, Skylar?"

My eyes cloud up. "I'm sorry," I repeat. "I'm crazy. I'm so crazy. I'm sorry."

He quickly sets a warm palm on my shoulder. "You're not crazy," he says firmly.

I swallow. "Will I have a new nurse?"

"Until Amelia gets well. But I'm not sure, she may be too afraid of you."

When he says that, my stomach plummets. "Doctor?"

"Yes?"

"What's wrong with me?"

His eyes turn soft. "There's nothing *wrong* with you," he tells me. "You're just ill."

"That's something wrong. I'm not supposed to be ill."

"We'll figure it out," he assures me, nodding. "But until then, you will have to be restrained." Then he nods to the food. It's new, of course, but the same meal as the one I had before. "But you will have to eat."

I frown, trying to pull my hands from the straps but failing. "I don't have any hands at the moment."

"I'll bring in a nurse to feed you," he tells me.

"Not Amelia?"

He sighs. "Not Amelia. See you tomorrow, Skylar." He turns and leaves and I'm left alone, tied to a bed. And I cry.

I'm hungry.

. . . .

The next day when I visit Mrs. Carter, my hands are tied as if I'm a prisoner, and Dr. Richards has to hold onto my arm the entire way there. It's humiliating.

When I enter the office, Mrs. Carter looks upset to see me, her eyes falling to the straps. Dr. Richards whispers something to her as I sit in the same love seat as always. Mrs. Carter nods politely. I glance down to the straps on my hands. They chafe against my skin.

The door shuts. Dr. Richards is gone.

"I heard you did something bad yesterday," Mrs. Carter says.

"I did," I admit.

"Why?"

I look up, my throat sore and my eyes foggy. "I don't know," I squeak.

She lets out a sigh. "What did she do to make you so angry?"

"She wanted me to eat."

"Is that all?"

I nod, but then I pause.

"Sky?"

I stare Mrs. Carter. "She asked me if I wanted to die," I murmur under my breath.

"And," Mrs. Carter begins slowly, surprise behind her eyes, "why did that upset you?"

I shrug.

"Skylar, *do* you want to die?"

That's when I begin to cry. I cry so hard, so loud, it hurts both my throat and my ears. Mrs. Carter sits there, allowing me to let it out. "I miss him," I moan.

I'm surprised at my words, and I'm so shocked I nearly stop crying. That was the first I had admitted I miss him. The first I mentioned him, too.

Mrs. Carter raises an eyebrow at this. "Who, Sky?"

I shake my head, closing my eyes.

"Who?"

"Nobody!" I snap. Tears still trickle, sliding down to my lips. I can taste the salt. Mrs. Carter hands me a tissue box and I take a few to blow my nose. "Thank you," I whisper.

Mrs. Carter nods as she waits for me to speak, but I never do. I just sit there sniffling, hair over my eyes, my head bowed, and my shoulders slouched. "Sky," she says at last, her voice thin. "Why do you want to die?"

I look up quickly. "I—" But I stop myself.

"I need to know, Skylar."

"I don't *want* to die," I finally tell her, lifting my head and pushing the hair from my eyes. "I don't want to kill myself. I won't kill myself."

She nods. "But are you depressed?"

I shrug. "Sometimes."

"About what?"

"Nothing in particular."

"Does *he* have anything to do with it?"

I almost ask what she means, meeting her curious expression, but then I remember I mentioned him. I sigh; I didn't ever want to mention him. I was supposed to forget about him because he wasn't real.… He wasn't real.… He.…

I hold my breath, forcing myself to stop. I need to stop. I see that Mrs. Carter can spot the struggle in my eyes. "I don't know," I whisper at last, glancing away from her. "I haven't even thought about him until today."

"But he obviously means something to you if you miss him."

"I didn't mean to say that," I whimper, pressing a strand of tangled curls behind my left ear.

"Who is he? I know he's not a nobody." Mrs. Carter's green eyes are warm, comforting. It's as if another world is beyond them. A world of peace. "Is he from your dream?" She clears her throat. "I mean… is he from that *place*?"

I nod.

"Would you feel better if you told me about him?"

I swallow, then shake my head.

"Well," she says, clearing her throat, "then how about you tell me more about what happened? We can ease into it. Together." She smiles.

I look up to the ceiling, that same sand color as the walls. Do I want to talk some more? I'm not sure. Especially about him. I don't know if I'd manage to get through. Maybe I can leave him out.

What am I saying? I know I can't leave him out.

Luckily I don't have to mention him just yet.

"Skylar?"

five

When I woke up again, I felt sick.

I checked all the rooms once more, looked out all the windows. I was still alone. It was still the same as before. But honestly, I didn't expect the streets to be crowded with pedestrians or taxis, nor did I expect Mom to be there. However, I had forgotten about the moss. I bit my lip, holding back my tears. I didn't know what to do. I wanted to call someone. I *needed* help. But it was just me. There was, evidently, nobody else.

I had a sour taste in my mouth, my stomach growing uneasy.

What was I supposed to do? Where was I supposed to go? I couldn't stay inside all my life and wait for Mom. Or maybe I could.

My stomach roared. I was absolutely famished. You aren't hungry in dreams, though. I knew that. And that terrified me all the more.

I went into the kitchen and turned on the coffee pot. I was never very good at making coffee because I was used to Mom making it all the time, but when I took a sip it wasn't bad, just a tad bit watery.

I made myself some cereal and sat at the table, eating slowly to pass the time, I guess. The ringing wasn't there, or at least wasn't as bad. But then again, I was chewing pretty loud, so I was probably just drowning it out.

I started crying then. Surprisingly, I missed my mom and I missed Andria. I missed everyone. Tears poured out thick from my burning eyes and my esophagus tightened. I wheezed and screamed. I had always been an ugly crier. I got that from Mom.

I wasn't aware of what time it was. Had I slept for an hour, a minute? Two days? Was it even the same day? I didn't know. But I did know that I was alone, and it was quiet.

After I ate and my sobs died down to mellow sniffs—I knew crying would get me absolutely nowhere—I went to a window again. I stared outside for a while, looking for a bird, a dog, a rat. Any sudden movement that might indicate life. And that's when I decided to leave the apartment.

I needed to find someone. I needed *answers*. There was obviously nothing out there; I was sure I'd be okay. But if there *was* a person out there, a person like me, maybe they'd see me from their apartment, or maybe I'd run into them on the streets. Maybe they'd know more than me and they'd help me find Mom.

I went to my room and found some leggings and a small, yellow T-shirt. I liked the color, but if Andria saw me wearing a yellow shirt, she'd kill me. I also grabbed my dad's gray athletic jacket, one of the only things he left behind. It was too big for me, but I liked it that way. I slipped on my favorite brown mountain boots and slicked my hair back into a messy ponytail. And at last, I stared into the mirror. I never thought of myself as pretty, but for some reason, at that moment I did. I looked like a tough kind of pretty. *If only people saw me now.* And besides, I thought I looked good in yellow.

Next, I grabbed a backpack and filled it with some granola bars, oranges, and water bottles, just in case I'd be gone for a few hours. I even grabbed my phone and its charger, just in case—and *duh*, I brought my headphones.

I sucked in my breath. Was I really going to do this? I wasn't sure if I wanted to. Well, of course I didn't want to; I didn't want any of this. I trembled, terrified of what I might find, or what I might *not* find. Maybe I didn't want to know what lay beyond those empty streets.

I slung the backpack over my shoulders, gnawing at the inside of my cheek until it bled. A bitter taste flooded my mouth and I cringed.

I made my way to the door of our apartment and held my breath. My tiny fingers reached for the knob and I grasped it tautly. I closed my eyes and hesitated before I cautiously opened the door; it *creeaaaaked* in a very eerie way. My heart raced wildly before I even saw what was behind it.

The hallway was utterly dark, and the wind hummed throughout the air. A chill fluttered down my spine as I chewed at my fingertips frantically.

"Crap," I mumbled as my eyes dilated to the never-ending shadows. I ran back inside and grabbed a flashlight from Mom's room. When I once again approached the hall, I turned the flashlight on. Nevertheless, the hallway remained absent of light. I sighed. Where were the lights? They had worked perfectly fine in our apartment.

I no longer wished to venture into the darkness, my bones trembling in fear. Gosh, I was so terrified. I had never done anything of this sort before, of course. I had never done anything exciting with my life—not that this was exciting, not in the general sense of the term. But my life had never consisted of anything dangerous; it consisted of books and shopping with Andria and googly-eyeing over the boys who walked by us at coffee shops. But there was nothing I could do about it at that moment. Whether I liked it or not, I *was* going outside.

I took one step and then another, holding my breath. The dim light of the flashlight bounced as my hands shook.

That was the last time I was in my apartment.

I walked carefully through the hall, knocking on the other doors as I did. You know, just to make sure. But it wasn't like anyone answered them.

I felt as though someone was watching me, their eyes staring hard at my back. I could almost hear their breath, feel their body heat. I kept glancing around, panicked, searching for those eyes I felt; although I knew I was alone, it never quite seemed that way. The wind sounded like the powerful cries of a famished wolf, but otherwise, the only thing I could hear were my quivering breaths.

It seemed hours later when I finally reached the end of the hall. I glanced to the elevator. I would prefer to take that since we're on the fourteenth floor, but I can't take any chances. If the elevator were to get stuck, I'd be screwed. So I decided to take the stairs, which were just as—maybe even a bit more—creepy as the hall. I gulped and began my journey downwards, making sure I set two feet on each step before I continued to the next, in case I'd miss one.

At last, I reached the lobby, which was dark as well, but besides that, it appeared the same as always.

The moment my eyes spotted the doors at the end of the lobby, my legs leapt from the stairs and I bolted toward the exit of the apartment complex. I was finished standing in the darkness, moving slowly.

I reached the doors and threw them open without hesitation, finally stepping outside.

I squinted, shading my eyes with one hand, the sun's rays coating me like second skin. I looked around the streets. They seemed almost emptier up close. And it was so bizarre; I felt so little standing in that big, open street. Perhaps I expected to see more, because my stomach plummeted when I realized there was nothing to be seen besides the buildings. And the moss.

What was I supposed to do? I hadn't really thought that through. I supposed I was just going to walk around, try to find somebody or something or, really, anything at all. I sighed, tugging my backpack straps. *Here goes nothing.* I told myself I wouldn't go back to the apartment until I found a sign of life—besides the trees and grass, of course. And I began to walk through the streets.

After a block or so, I started calling out, "Hello?" Quiet at first, then louder. I ended up screaming it, cupping my lips with my palms. "Hello! Hello! Is anyone out there?" Nobody answered, but that was pretty obvious, right? It would be cliché if someone called back, "I'm here!" from their apartment window.

I had walked through the city for about an hour when I gave up. Sitting on the curb of the street, I pressed my hands to my eyes and slouched over. I didn't cry, but I wanted to. However, with my throat sore from my screaming and my anxiety keeping me still, I did not dare cry.

I was thirsty, so I fetched a water bottle from the bag and gulped down a few sips. Wiping my mouth with the back of my hand, I looked up, my eyes traveling down an alleyway. To my surprise, I saw something at the end. A figure. Some sort of animal. I closed my eyes tight and shook my head, but when I opened them again it was still there.

Only it was walking toward me.

I quickly stood up, grasping the water bottle tightly, my breaths shaky again. I narrowed my eyes, trying to figure out what it was. I was so hopeful to find life, and of course, as soon as I found it I was absolutely terrified.

I stepped back a few steps, not that it'd make any difference.

The thing was so close then I could see it clearly. I realized it was a cat, with four legs and four mighty paws. It was gold—like actually made out of gold, slick and glimmering beneath the light, with bright emerald eyes. The nearer it was to me the bigger I realized it was. Probably ten feet tall... no, wait, eleven. Thirteen? And for some reason, I was no longer scared; I was mesmerized, its long tail whipping behind it.

The cat resembled a female lion, strong and brilliant. She lifted her head high, strolling toward me in such a way that made her seem the leader of the city. She owned the place. She was trying to tell me that, I figured. Was I supposed to stand my ground?

She halted in front of me, bowing her head to look at me curiously, yet it seemed as though she already knew who I was. What I was. She had seen me before.

You aren't supposed to be here, she purred within my head, her voice soft yet somewhat stern. I gasped, dropping the water bottle and pressing my palms to my ears. Had she spoken to me through my head? *Yes.*

My eyes met hers, widened and afraid. "Who are you?"

I would like to ask you the same question. Her voice still felt funny in my mind.

I bit my bottom lip. Unbelievable. Impossible. "I thought you could read my mind," I whispered.

She raised her head just a bit, swinging her tail. It took her a bit to respond, and I swear I felt another being in my mind for just a split second. *Yes,* her voice echoed within, at last. *I know who you are. And you shouldn't be here.*

I swallowed. "And here would be…?"

She didn't reply, only stared.

"H-hello?"

You need to go back.

My lips parted, but no sound came out.

You need to leave. This is my city now.

I frowned, completely unsure of what was happening. "Who—"

Leave.

"But I—"

Leave!

I stepped back quickly, my hands trembling at my side. I didn't know what to do. Was I supposed to just leave? She didn't frighten me; she barely even looked real. But her voice in my head unsettled me, as I'm sure it would to most.

I knew she wouldn't let me stay; I had to go back. But, go back where? What did she mean? Of course, my fear controlled my actions, and my feet stayed planted on the ground. I couldn't move. I was too *afraid* to move. But at the same time, I wasn't scared at all.

Next thing I knew, two more cats appeared at her side from the other alleyways. They were smaller, and not as intimidating. She was obviously the leader.

She took a step forward, her paw clicking firm against the cement of the street. Bowing her head, she stared at me so intensely that I shivered from the force. She was dominating the land. It *was* her city. It was no longer mine.

That's when my feet finally unglued themselves from the street and I ran away. They chased me, running quite elegantly behind, and amazingly fast. It was so freaking terrifying.

I don't run. I never run. I ran in P.E. sometimes, and in soccer when I was, like, five. But besides that, I've never ran… at least never like this. I never do *anything* active besides window shopping in the mall. So that running, it wasn't fun. My chest tightened, my throat quickly grew dry, and I felt the sweat dripping beneath my dad's athletic jacket. I was sprinting I think, rather than actually running, for the cats moved so swiftly compared to me. They were right on my heels, and I could feel their metallic breath on the back of my neck. I couldn't slow down or else who knew what they'd do to me. I ran, breathing so loudly it was nearly the only thing I could hear.

I dashed through alleyways and streets, passing by the shops and business properties I usually saw every day… just under different circumstances, of course. It was odd, and part of me sometimes forgot I was running from giant golden cats; besides the moss covering everything, the shops and businesses seemed pretty normal, just as they did every day before then.

But then suddenly, I reached an opening in the city which I didn't know was there before. I saw miles and miles of beautiful greenery, with a simple stone road extending into the openness. I halted before it. They had chased me to this. Was this where I was supposed to leave?

I turned and noticed the cats had stopped as well. They stood quietly, their faces soft, not as frightening. They didn't look even the least bit tired from all that running, while I was panting wildly, my ponytail falling apart, and my cheeks flushed.

The leader nodded to the opening. *Leave,* she said, her voice gentle again.

But I couldn't just *leave.* What if Mom came back to the apartment, realized I was gone? Wouldn't she be worried? But I had my phone with me. Maybe she'd call. But then I swallowed thickly, knowing such a thing wouldn't happen. Why? Because there before me stood those giant, golden cats. And everyone else was gone.

"Where am I supposed to go?" I asked the cats softly, as if they hadn't just nearly killed me.

You'll know, she assured me, nodding again and flicking her tail. The cat to her right sat down and closed its eyes as if it were tired, the only one who appeared so. *You have to go back. You are not supposed to be here.*

I gave her a quick nod. Then I turned and began to walk away on the road, utterly confused yet excited to discover what lay beyond the green. I had never seen so much before at once, as I had never really left the city. Only once, really, but that was forever ago.

I didn't know if I was ready to leave, however. Leave Mom, Andria, Matt. Leave my life, the one I had always known. But if I stayed there, who knew what the cats would do to me.

Farewell, Skylar Vail, the leader purred. The way she said my name made me shudder, and I turned to look at her over my shoulder. It appeared as though she were smiling. *Good luck.*

Surprisingly I smiled back. It was without teeth, my lips thin and barely curled, but I still considered it a smile. Then I turned my head back, my gaze traveling into the unknown, and I began to walk forward, out into the green. Who knew how far the road went. A car definitely would have been helpful.

I felt the cats staring at my frail body until I'd walked for about half an hour. When I no longer felt their emerald eyes, I looked back to see that the city was no longer visible. It was nothing but a slender, black shadow amongst the distance. There was no turning back.

Oh, crap.

six

I hate being restrained. It's even more boring than having my hands free. But luckily it stops me from biting my nails raw, as I tend to do in here. Perhaps I can finally quit the habit.

Talking about the world is strange, and I'm not so sure I like it yet. I sound so stupid when I say it, because it's as if it really was just a dream, and I'm really just going crazy. But who am I kidding? Of course I'm going crazy. I've been going crazy since the start.

I stare at the wall before me, remembering the cats. I miss them, actually. I wonder how they're doing.

. . . .

I don't talk for the next three sessions. I think I'm trying to avoid talking about him, but I don't know why, really. And I think Mrs. Carter can tell, yet she doesn't question my absence of voice. She just sits, allowing me to look at the wall and think about the beach, my hands tied in my lap. I did tell Mrs. Carter I was getting a rash from the straps. She said she'd talk to Dr. Richards, but he hasn't done anything about it, so I don't really think she did.

But once the fourth day comes around, Mrs. Carter finally questions my silence. "You were talking just fine before," she says. "Why are you having a difficult time now?"

I shrug.

"You should let out your emotions, Skylar. What are you feeling inside?"

I frown, for I am not entirely sure. Am I sad? Worried? Scared? Do I feel exposed? Do I feel alone? How am I supposed to know?

When I don't answer immediately, she answers for me. "I think you feel like you can't tell me things." I look up at her, meeting her hard stare. Her red hair is up today in a tight bun, and she wears skinny jeans, a bright yellow blouse, and heels. She always wears heels. Today, they are slick and black and shiny. My eyes drift down to them.

"Hello? Is that true?"

I shrug again.

"Skylar, look at me." I look at her. "You don't think I've had guy problems, too?"

I frown, raising an eyebrow. *What does she mean by a guy problem? Where does she figure I'm sad because of a boy?* Ridiculous.

But I guess it's partially true.

No, it's very much true.

"Skylar, let me tell you a story. Okay?"

"Okay," I agree.

She swallows, adjusting herself in the chair. "One time, when I was about your age, I think, I met a boy." She cringes as she remembers. "He was the new boy at school, wildly handsome and kind. He was in three of my classes." She smiles a sad smile. "I went up to him, asked him where he was from. And I ended up showing him around the school that same day."

Her eyes appear downcast, nearly brimming with tears.

"Next thing you know, we ended up going out to dinner. Like, as a date," she continued. "He picked me up and took me somewhere special, even when he was new and had no clue where anything was! But he insisted on taking me. He was *so* sweet, and we had much in common. I *really* liked him. And he was the first boy I ever kissed." She breathes in deep, her eyes flicking to the wall beside her. "We'd been going out for a month when one day he didn't answer the phone. He didn't show up to school for two days, either. I thought, 'Is he mad at me? Did I say something? Is he sick?' Eventually, I went to his house, but I saw the for-sale sign. They had gone. He had left me without even saying good-bye, as if he were never even there."

She sniffs, wiping her glistening eyes; she still isn't over it. But she turns back to me, smiling again, and this time actually appearing happy. "I still get sad telling the story, but I'm not as heartbroken as I once was. He never called me again. I never found out where he went. Stuff like that... you never quite heal because all your life, you believe it was *your* fault. I haven't seen him in about fifteen years, and I *swear*, we were soul mates. But perhaps... perhaps not."

She shakes her head, her smile subsiding. "Skylar," she says, looking me in the eye. "Sometimes boys leave with no explanation. People of all sorts leave with no explanation. And sadly we have no control over that. It just happens. *Poof,* they're gone." She laughs at that. "It hurts a lot, and our heart cracks and our lips quiver and our eyes get all misty, but sooner or later, we *have* to get over it. We have to let go. There's no use in missing someone who left you because whether it was you or whether it was them, it wasn't meant to be, and somehow the other person realized that sooner than you did."

I swallow. "You don't seem over it though, Mrs. Carter."

She grins. "Skylar, nobody really gets over it. At least not all the way, that is. But we do get stronger, wiser... and we do find something better." She breathes in, her eyes cold. Nevertheless, she manages a smile. "We always do. We always will."

I smile. "Thank you, Mrs. Carter."

"Oh, please call me Susan, would you? I just like it better."

I find myself giggling. "Okay, Susan."

"Now," she begins, her voice suddenly flat, "are you ready to talk about the boy?" I look away. "Are you ready to let it go?"

I'm about to open my mouth, about to tell her... but then I stop myself. "No," I snap. "I'm not. And I never will be."

Mrs. Carter stares at me blankly, and I give her a sneer.

. . . .

I cried so hard that night. April fifteenth. I remember the day well, much too well.

My first heartbreak.

Andria held me as we sat on the floor of my room, and I sobbed and bawled and clenched my fists. "I hate him!" I wailed. "I hate him so much!"

"Why?" Andria asked, so softly I barely heard.

"For making me feel this way."

"Don't let him make you feel this way," she said.

"How? How do I stop the pain?" I opened my eyes and stared at her, waiting for a reply. She appeared so calm, so peaceful.

"You *don't* stop it."

"It hurts so much, Andria. So. Freaking. Much."

"Don't let it hurt."

"How?" Tears fell from my eyes, stinging, salty on my skin.

"You're stronger than this, Sky. You're stronger than the feelings and you're stronger than his words. You deserve better. You deserve more."

"It still hurts," I whimpered.

She sighed, petting my hair and pulling me closer. "I know, Sky. I know."

I grabbed her shirt and sobbed on her shoulder.

"Just cry," she said. "Cry it out, okay?"

So of course, I did. And she stayed with me until I stopped, which was not until a week later.

. . . .

That night, I have a dream.

I hadn't really gone to sleep since the happening, for I am afraid to go to sleep, to accidentally get stuck in the world again. I lay awake at night, forcing my eyes to stay open. Sometimes I drift in and out of consciousness, but I always try to keep myself busy, or my mind, that is. I always try to stay awake.

But tonight, I accidently close my eyes a little too long. I feel my fingers grow numb, and I can no longer control my body. And before I know it I'm standing in an empty hall, like the one in the apartment building. I cannot see, for it is dark. I cannot breathe. I grasp my throat, gulping the freezing air like a pure drink of water.

A light flickers on and there he stands. He looks so handsome, as always. Tall, intimidating, yet there is an evident gentle side to him. His green eyes stare into mine and he smiles, so relaxed, as if he were obviously expecting to see me.

"Skylar," he says my name, his voice as deep as the depths of the dark blue ocean. My insides melt.

I try to walk to him, but my feet don't move; I'm stuck, drenched in confusion. I still can't breathe, either.

He strolls my way, hands at ease, head tilted to the side as he studies me. Once he is close, I can smell his minty breath, feel his body heat extending to me like warm, comforting hands. He cups my face with a palm, and I can feel him. He's so real. He's there.

"I miss you," he murmurs.

I try to say something back, but my voice won't work and my lips refuse to part.

"I'm still looking," he says firmly. "But don't worry, I'm close."

I can't touch him. I can't grab his hand. I can't kiss him. I want to scream but, of course, I *can't*.

He removes his hand from my jaw and begins walking backward. *Don't go,* I try to screech. *Please, stay.* But he can't hear my thoughts, and he supposedly can't see my struggle.

"I won't stop looking," he calls, smiling. "I promise. I will never break my promise. I'll see you again soon, Skylar."

Then the lights turn completely off again and I'm left alone.

I'm abandoned.

I'm confused.

And I'm forsaken.

seven

"I need Mrs. Carter," I say to the young nurse on the other side of the phone. The room phone is at my side, on speaker. Don't even ask me how I was able to grab it while being restrained. Let's just say that my arms are completely coated in bloody rashes, but if Mrs. Carter comes, it'll all be worth it.

"Skylar?" the nurse asks, her voice sweet, like pink and yellow candy. She sounds too young to be a nurse. "Skylar Vail?"

"Yes," I say.

"Um… it's two in the morning. Why are you awake?"

"That's why I need Mrs. Carter."

"Well, sweetie, I don't know," she murmurs. "She's probably asleep right now. Why do you need her?"

"Please," I beg before my words tumble out fast. "I need to talk to her. Just call her, okay? At least maybe she can call me back, or maybe tell me something through you."

"Okay, Skylar, but—"

"*Please*," I cry. "I had a scary dream, and I can feel him watching me still. I'm afraid and I don't want to stay in here alone. Mrs. Carter will know what to do. *Please*, I'm *begging* you."

I can hear the nurse suck in a deep breath, thinking. "All right," she tells me. "I'll call her, honey. But I'm afraid I'm not completely sure if she'll answer. Usually—"

"Thank you," I say.

. . . .

Mrs. Carter walks into the room, the opened door bringing in a bit of light from the hall outside. It was completely dark before then; they shut the blinds every night.

"You okay, Skylar?" she asks in a sleepy voice.

She's about to turn on the lights when I say abruptly, "No, I like the dark."

Her thin fingers slowly lower from the light switch. "Okay," she whispers. She walks over to the bathroom in the room. "But I have to turn on *some* light." She flicks it on and leaves the door open just a crack. I see then that she wears polar bear pajama pants much too big for her and a gray tank top with a big, pink robe hanging from her bony shoulders. I don't think she wears a bra. And her red hair is up in a messy bun, her face fresh and clean with no makeup. She looks young like this... like a teenage girl, actually. No, maybe twenty. But either way she looks a lot prettier without makeup. "I came here as fast as I could," she tells me.

I can't actually believe that she came. I thought maybe she'd call me. Honestly, I thought she wouldn't even answer the phone. But here she is, in her pj's.

"I should get coffee," she says, smiling. Her eyes look smaller. "Would you like some coffee?"

Coffee. The last time I had coffee, it was the first day in that world. I lick my lips. I can already taste it. "Am I allowed to have coffee?" Coffee is the first thing that has actually sounded good to have since I've been here.

"Probably not… not at this hour anyway," she laughs. "But it'll be my treat." She winks and leaves the room. She's back in a few minutes with two cups of coffee and two blueberry muffins on a tray in a rolling chair. She pushes the chair to the side of the bed, and then her eyes find my wrists and her light expression becomes appalled. "Oh my," she gasps. "What happened?"

"I was trying to call the nurse," I say flatly.

She shakes her head. "This is ridiculous," she says under her breath. Then she stares at me. "What if you have to go to the bathroom?"

"I have to call a nurse."

She frowns.

"I normally hold it in, though. It's okay. I don't eat much, you know. Or drink."

"I'm going to have to talk to the doctors about this," she snaps. "This is *ridiculous.*"

"You said that already," I murmur.

She laughs and begins undoing the straps.

"Mrs. Carter—"

"Susan," she corrects.

"*Susan*," I say. "I threw a metal tray at a nurse and knocked her out because she wanted me to eat." I expect her to stop undoing the straps, but she doesn't. She doesn't seem to have heard what I just said. "I threw a *tray* at a—"

"I know," she barks, glancing up to me for just a moment. "But she also brought feelings into it and she shouldn't have. She doesn't know what is going through your head. Neither do I, but I have a better idea. And she doesn't need to get inside your head—nobody does. Well, I guess I do because I'm a counselor, so I'm *allowed* to ask death questions and stuff. It's my job. Not hers." She smiles. "It was her fault... kind of." One strap becomes loose and I yank my hand back. It feels so nice to once again have free wrists, and I can't help but grin.

"Are you even allowed to do this?" I ask.

"No," she laughs. "But oh well." She starts undoing the other strap.

"What if I throw a tray at you?"

"Then," she sighs, "I'm kind of screwed, aren't I?" She grins at me. "I guess I'll just have to hope you don't throw a tray at me."

I almost laugh. "Why did you come?"

"Oh, Sky. If you need me, I'll be here."

"But don't you have to be here tomorrow...." I pause to think about it. "Or later today, I mean?"

She nods. "But that's okay. I'm always here."

"You don't take days off?"

She shrugs. "Only occasionally. I don't go home much." The second strap is free and I feel a weight being lifted off my chest, which is funny because the weight was on my wrist.

Mrs. Carter moves the tray from the chair onto my lap, taking her coffee and muffin from it.

"You can have my muffin," I tell her.

"Nonsense," she says. "These muffins will change your *life*."

I smirk. "Well, okay." I pick up the coffee cup and take a nice, warm sip, and I can feel the sweet liquid flowing through my skin. I shiver.

"Do you need bandages for your wrists?" Mrs. Carter asks, sitting in the rolling chair. I shake my head. "Okay." She sips on her coffee for a second. "So, what is it?"

"Him," I find myself say, my voice trembling.

"Oh, I see," she replies. "Would you like to talk about it?"

"I'm not sure," I mumble.

"Skylar," she sighs, "why are you so afraid of him?"

I frown, meeting her green eyes. "I'm not *afraid* of him."

"Yes," she says, nodding, "you are. Why? Did he hurt you?"

"No!" I snap. "He…." I breathe in, closing my eyes. I think of his face, his smile… his kiss. I open my eyes, looking about the room before I turn to her again. "I *love* him."

"Ah," she says slowly. "Love is a strong word."

"I'm aware," I murmur.

"Are you afraid of falling in love with him all over again?"

"No."

"Skylar?"

I sigh. "Yes, I am."

"Why?"

"Because I need to get over him. I'll probably never see him again."

I want Mrs. Carter to tell me otherwise. Tell me, "No, don't think like that, Skylar! Of course you'll see him again!" Instead she nods, crossing her legs and taking a bite out of her muffin. "You should try it," she tells me with her mouth full, tilting her head toward mine.

I set my coffee cup on the tray and pick up my muffin, taking a small bite of it. It's really good. I chew, swallow, and realize how hungry I am, taking three more big bites.

Mrs. Carter giggles. "Told you."

"Susan," I say.

"Hm?"

"You remind me of my best friend."

She smiles. "I'm glad, honey. Why?"

"She's always all over the place," I say with a smirk. "And she's happier. She's bubbly, and kind, and always knows what to say."

"Happier," Mrs. Carter repeats. "Happier than you?"

I nod. "That's why we're friends. My usual cold self balances out when I'm around her."

She nods. "Well, I'm glad I'm like her."

"Mrs. Car—" I clear my throat quickly. "Susan," I correct. "I think I want to tell you about when I saw Tristan."

"Oh?" Her eyebrow rises and her eyes are filled with sudden excitement.

I nod. "It'll help."

She grins. "Just pretend like I'm your best friend."

I smile because Andria and I are no longer friends, due to what happened between us before *it* happened... before I went crazy. So right now, Mrs. Carter is my best friend. I guess that's kind of sad; my counselor is my current best friend. But that makes it easier, so I guess it's good, too.

I take one last sip of my coffee, and then I tell her amidst the dark, yet welcoming shadows of the room.

eight

I walked down the lonely road, into the emptiness, the openness. I felt as though I was literally the only one left in the world, or at least in *that* world, and perhaps I was. I had decided that that place certainly wasn't the same place I had grown up in. I was sure of that. I just had to figure out how to get home, and by the look of it, the road wasn't doing me any good. I had strolled upon it for miles, thirsty and hungry. I had eaten all of my granola bars, so all I had left were my two oranges. There was no food in sight besides grass. No water, either. I drank an entire water bottle already, so I had one left. I wasted the other one by dropping it on the street. I sighed, this didn't look so good.

Once I began thinking of the oranges, I remembered that I had my phone, *and* my headphones. How could I have forgotten? I stopped and shuffled through my bag, pulling them both out and putting the earbuds in my ears before slipping my phone into the pocket of Dad's athletic jacket. I went to my music, which consisted of nothing but Weezer, Coldplay, and a few 60's songs my mom liked. Oh, and there were a few random songs by people like Britney Spears or AWOLNATION, but it was *mostly* Coldplay, which has *always* been my favorite. I turned on the song "Strawberry Swing" and continued walking. The familiar melody hummed in my mind, soothing my tense body, and for just a split second, I felt at home again. Everything was normal, as though nothing had ever changed. I closed my eyes, very thankful the music still worked.

I imagined myself somewhere else, like still in bed, or at school. I imagined the city streets crammed with people. I had always hated the overpopulation of the city, the lights and the noise. But right then I just wanted it all back.

I opened my eyes and realized how truly beautiful the scenery was. All that green. Of course, it wasn't what I would've liked to see, but it was certainly a pretty sight. A sight I didn't mind, at least.

My feet fell into the rhythm of the music. Somehow, amidst all the craziness, I actually felt at peace.

Until I saw another figure in front of me.

Although, this figure was different. It seemed to be a person, lying right in the center of the road, not too far ahead. I paused. Hesitated.

What if it's another cat? That would suck.

But in the very pit of my stomach, I felt something I hadn't felt before—not in that world, that is. A warmth spread throughout my body, and I smiled. I think it was hope. *If it is a person, then perhaps they can help me!* I didn't even think about the dangers… or not much of them. I was just excited; I had *at last* found a person, at least I most likely had.

I began running toward the figure, the headphones falling out of my ears. It was a man. Well, he seemed smaller than a man, actually. But I didn't care; it was a *person*.

He was lying on his side, his back toward me. He looked like he'd be a greaser or something with his leather jacket and blue jeans, Converses, and messy brown hair. I don't know why I thought of that then but I did. What a random comparison.

"Hello?" I asked, raising a hand in defense, just in case. But he didn't reply. I supposed he was asleep, so I walked around his limp body until I saw his face.

He was absolutely breathtaking, and probably seventeen or so. His eyes were closed and he looked at peace—and comfortable, despite his position on the cement road. His face was pale like mine, and his jaw was clean-cut, like fresh stone. His skin was smooth and looked to be amazingly soft. I nearly reached out and touched it, but instead I stood and admired him.

Before long, my mind awoke once again and I could think clearly. Of course, I was happy; the only other person in this world, or so it seemed, happened to be a very attractive guy, somewhat around my age. It was so cliché, though. *So* cliché. I could see now why you'd think this would all be a dream, because nothing like this occurs in real life; I'm afraid people just don't have that sort of luck. Yet, apparently I did.

Suddenly, I noticed a puddle of red leaking from beneath him. I panicked and lifted his shirt without hesitation, trying my hardest not to stare. On the side he was lying on was a huge, deep gash. I didn't know what I was supposed to do. He obviously needed stitches, but I didn't know how to do that, nor did I have the supplies—not even a bandage!

But then I paused. Was he breathing? I checked for a pulse, and my stomach plummeted when I didn't find it at first. Eventually I did, albeit a faint one, and I began breathing again. I wondered what had happened to him, what had done so much damage.

I had an idea then. I carefully slid his jacket off, making sure not to bump the gash and cause him any pain, even though he was asleep. As I did this, I noticed he had scratches on his arms, and if I looked closely enough, I could see the thin lines in his jacket as well.

What did this?

I fetched my last water bottle and gently poured it over the wound, hoping it'd lower his chances of an infection. I propped him up on my knee, tightly tying the jacket around his waist, most of the leather pressed against the gash. After situating the two of us, I looked down at him, his pale face. He had such a mysterious attractiveness to him. He seemed to be the type to be cruel and cold, the typical bad boy. But then again, there was a kindness to him unlike any other; just looking at him, I could tell. He didn't know he was nice, yet he was. He had a charm that he didn't exactly know about. And *man*, was he beautiful.

I decided to quit walking then. The sun had already begun to set, and I was mentally and physically exhausted from this long, confusing, and terrifying day. I set the boy down on the grass beside me and plugged my headphones back in, staring out at the endless green while listening to "Clocks" by Coldplay. I slowly drifted away, eventually lying down against the grass, and gently closing my eyes. I felt the warm melody spread throughout me and I was soon going to sleep, thinking of the day that had just occurred: The silence, the cats, and the green... the boy. *What was the purpose of this? Where the heck am I? Why is this happening to...?*

I fell asleep to those thoughts.

. . . .

I woke up and it was dark, the moon big and bright, its light creating a white puddle across my feet. There was no other light besides that ... everything was still, and silent. The air was frosty in my lungs, and everything was cold. And then I heard screeches in the distance and my body stiffened.

I reached over for the boy, my body trembling, but he wasn't there. I frowned, searching for my phone and headphones, but they weren't there either ... everything was gone. I began to panic, my breaths fast and my heart beat quick. The boy had left and stolen my things.

I was alone again.

I was mad at myself. No matter how handsome he was, I knew I shouldn't have trusted him enough to fall asleep beside him, but I did anyway, and I was robbed.

I heard the screeches again. They sounded like they belonged to the undead, loud and piercing and sad. I was too frightened to cry.

I stood up quickly, finding the cement of the road with my feet. And once I did, I noticed dribbles of blood beneath the bold illumination of the moon. I looked up from the road, biting my lip, searching out into the darkness. And then I descended into the unknown at a quick yet hesitant pace. Of course, I wanted to find him because I wanted my things back, especially my music. Not because he was incredibly attractive....

The screeches grew louder, closer. I heard movement in the grass, but under the dim moonlight I couldn't see a thing. I couldn't tell what the screeches belonged to but I knew it wasn't good, so I began running.

There were footsteps behind me on the road, and what sounded like crazed laughter. My mind couldn't process what was happening, so I wouldn't say I was scared. I was kind of lost and confused. It felt like a dream, where everything was a blur and didn't feel real. But my instincts forced me to run anyway because I did know that something was chasing me. Or some *things*.

I followed the droplets, my feet hitting against the cement fast and hard, creating a *clonk* type sound. I could hear more things join the chase behind me, so I ran faster. I was actually getting used to running; my chest didn't burn as much, and my throat wasn't as tight. But it was still running, so it wasn't comfortable, of course.

My entire body ached, my left side was gnawing it's way to my stomach and the soles of my feet screeching in agony. The creatures screamed and howled behind me, quickly nearing my vulnerable body.

Suddenly, beneath the light of the moon, I saw a house not too far away. It was a small, one-story wooden cabin … completely random among the current scenery.

I made my way toward it, and as soon as I was close enough to put my hand on the knob, I pulled open the door and ran inside, pressing my back against the door and closing it swiftly. The creatures banged against it from the outside, screeching and hollering to get inside, to eat me alive. And that's when the tears fell. I was so afraid that, in that moment, I realized it wasn't a dream. I cried and cried, screamed, "GO AWAY! LEAVE! STOP IT!" to the creatures.

And that's when the boy appeared from the kitchen. I barely even saw him he sped past me so fast, but I recognized the leather jacket. "Move!" he yelled as he ran toward the door. I flew out of the way, utterly surprised and confused, landing smack down against the floor. I turned to face him, using my arms to hold myself up, and watched as the boy threw open the door, brandishing a flashlight. It wasn't mine from the bag he stole; this one was much brighter and bigger. I still couldn't see the creatures completely, despite the bright glow, but I did see decaying forms quickly shrivel away and fleed, crying out in pain as if the light were burning them.

My lips were parted in complete shock as I watched the boy. The light reflected against his face and I stared at him. He looked much older awake… too old for me to be attracted to him, even.

Once the screeches calmed and at last disappeared, he shut the door. The flashlight was still on, and he set it on a coffee table near me before twisting around his head and fixing his eyes on mine. They were green, like freshly cut grass, brilliant and intense. His expression was hard, and he seemed annoyed with me. *Very* annoyed. But besides that, he appeared the same as when I fell asleep beside him on the grass, with the jacket tied tightly around his waist, scratches on his arms, and dried blood on his jeans.

"What were you thinking?" he asked me with a deep voice… deep like the depths of the ocean. And actually quite harsh.

"Uh…." I lifted an eyebrow, my breaths still quick and my mind still consumed by fear. "*Excuse* me?"

"You could've killed me!"

I frowned. "But I didn't?"

He sighs. "Whatever."

"Um, okay," I mumbled, standing up and rubbing my left elbow, sore from hitting the ground during the fall. "Nice to meet you, too?" I paused. "Wait. You stole from me. Where is my phone?"

He shrugged. "I don't know."

I took a step toward him. "What do you mean, 'I don't know'? Where *is* it?"

"Is that my blood on your boots?" he asked, nodding to my feet.

"What?"

"Your boots." I looked down at them and noticed they had dots and splatters of red across the front. "Ew," he spat.

"I followed the trail," I said, my eyes slowly rising back up to meet his.

"*Ew*." He cringed.

"You should be thanking me," I snapped.

"Huh?"

"If it weren't for me, you would have bled out and died right there on that road."

"No, I'm pretty sure I would've done okay on my own. Tying my jacket around my waist wasn't, like, the smartest thing to do."

"*Well*," I mumbled defensively, "I was short on supplies!"

"You had a lot in your bag."

"Yeah, some oranges and a flashlight!"

"And a phone."

"Where the heck is my *stuff*?" I paused. "Wait, before that... did the bleeding stop?"

"What?"

"Your wound. Has it stopped bleeding?"

His face grew plain. He looked down and moved the jacket, lifting his shirt to reveal the wound. It was no longer bleeding, and when he noticed, he nodded.

"Okay, good," I said, grinning. "So it did stop from the jacket."

"Yeah, just *now* it did. It bled the entire way here. And by the way, I'm pretty sad about my jacket. It was my favorite, and now it's covered in blood. You *ruined* it. So, thanks."

"No problem." My eyes drifted about the house as I pressed a strand of loose red hair behind my right ear. "How long have you been here?" I asked, admiring the cleanliness of the house.

"For, like, three hours, I think?" He began to move the jacket back over his wound.

"And you haven't bandaged yourself yet?"

He pressed his lips into a line. "I didn't even think of that."

"It needs to be cleaned and bandaged. I'll help you."

He frowned. "Why the hell do you want to help me?"

"What do you mean?"

"I stole your stuff."

"True," I said, sealing my lips tightly. "I'll just let it get infected, and I'll let you *die*, because you're a thief."

"Oh, geez. Okay then."

"I'm *kidding*," I laughed, more powerfully than I shoud've. "I'll go find bandages."

"But *why* are you helping me?"

"'Cause you need me," I told him as I headed into the kitchen. "And I need you. You obviously know a bit more about this place than me. You shined that flashlight on those things and they disappeared before my eyes, for example." I opened a few drawers and shuffled through them until I found little Hello Kitty Band-Aids. I needed bigger ones than that, obviously.

The boy appeared at my side. I turned to him and held up the bandages. "Do you like Hello Kitty?" He smirked. "No, but really." My face grew serious. "How did you know those things would go away with light?" His face grew cold and he looked away. "As a matter of fact, how do you even know what those things are?" I paused. "Wait. Did *they* give you the gash?"

He looked into my eyes, his own green ones alight. "I've been here for a while. They go away once the sun rises and appear as soon as the sun sets. I figured they hated light, so I kind of just risked both our lives to shine a flashlight on them. But it worked."

I noticed he avoided my last question, but then again, I avoided asking him why. "Indeed it did," I said. "But if you knew that, why did you leave me there on the street? Why did you rob me? If you knew I helped you…." I glance away for a second before returning my gaze to his. "Why did you leave?"

"I don't know. Sorry about that." He sighed. "I'm just kind of scared, I guess."

"You're not the only one in this world who's scared," I spat.

"So I guess that means you're scared too? Yeah, I figured as much from your expression when I saw you standing against the door."

I frowned, then continued shuffling through drawers.

"I'm sorry," he said. I could tell he meant it, his deep voice softening. "From now on, I won't leave you on the side of the road, okay?"

"Can you bring the flashlight over? I can barely see a thing."

He nodded, left, and then returned with the flashlight. I searched the cabinets and fetched the rubbing alcohol.

He whistled. "Gosh, that's going to hurt."

"Yeah, it probably will."

"I said I'm sorry," he snapped.

"And I heard you. Where is the bedroom? I need a shirt: I can't find any bandages, at least not big ones."

"Down the hall," he said, tilting his head to the nearest hallway.

"Thanks," I replied, taking the flashlight from him before adding, "I'll be right back." I left and strolled down the hall into the first room on the right. Heading into the closet, I picked out a big green T-shirt, which was thin and soft. I walked back down the hall, to see the boy sitting at the kitchen table, his face in his hands. "You okay?" I asked.

He looked up quickly, his eyes wide. "You startled me."

"Sorry," I replied flatly as I began shuffling through drawers until I found scissors. I walked to the boy then, picking up the rubbing alcohol and sitting next to him at the table, positioning the flashlight to shine on his chest. "Lift your shirt," I told him.

"Well, thirsty now, aren't you?" he asked me with a flirty sneer.

"Actually, I am. Now, lift your shirt."

"I'm sure they have water here."

"But the lights don't work?"

"Suppose not." He lifted his shirt, but then he ended up taking the entire thing off, revealing his bare upper body. My heart pounded in my chest. He leaned back into the chair, and I scooted mine toward him.

"You better hold on tight to the chair," I said to him softly. "This may sting."

I grabbed a napkin from the table, dribbled a little rubbing alcohol on it, and lifted it above the ugly wound. "Three… two… one." His grasp on the chair tightened as I pressed the napkin gently to the gash and he screamed out so loud, my ear drums numbing. I squinted until he stopped. "Shhhh," I whispered. "I'm sorry." I opened my eyes and I swear I saw him crying. His green eyes met mine, wild and in pain. I reached out to him, gently grasping his bare shoulder. "It's okay. I just have to do this a few more times."

"*What?*" he hissed. "*Crap.*"

After each successive dab of rubbing alcohol, the boy didn't scream as loud, but by the last one there were real tears running down his face. I thought it was cute and I blushed, passing him a napkin to wipe them away. "Okay," I told him. "I'm done."

Funny what a guy can do to a girl in an abandoned world with killer, night creatures.

I fetched the scissors, cutting the T-shirt in half. I stretched it out, wrapping it around his waist and over the wound, fairly tightly but not so much where it'd be uncomfortable. I grabbed the other half and did the same, tying them together.

"Thank you," he breathed. I nodded. "You're really good at this."

"Really?" I laughed. "I've never done it before." I bit my bottom lip, meeting his eyes. "What did this to you, anyway?"

He took a deep breath, his eyes flicking away. "I don't even know. I don't remember. Probably some kind of wild thing that didn't like me very much."

After the T-shirt was secure, we went into the kitchen, fetched some water bottles and Cheez-Its and Oatmeal Cream Pies, and transitioned to the couch. We sat on opposite sides, silently eating and drinking, gazing out into the darkness. The flashlight was still in the kitchen.

The familiar silence crept over me like a frosty chill and I shivered. I reached behind me and pulled a blanket over my frail body. The quiet stung my ears, but I didn't know how to start a conversation.

That's when I heard the screeches again from outside. I met the boy's eyes and he carefully lifted a finger to his lips to tell me to be silent, as if I weren't before. I currently had a Cheez-It in my mouth, but I didn't dare chew anymore.

For at least five minutes, we didn't hear any more screeches, so I whispered, "Will they come back?"

"Maybe, but if so, we'll be ready." He seemed so sure.

I nodded. "But how will I know you don't leave tomorrow?"

"Huh?"

I took a bite of an Oatmeal Cream Pie. "Leave me again, steal my things."

"'Cause we're a team," he said with a sly smile.

"A team?" I repeated, smirking, my mouth full.

"Of course."

"When did we become a team? I don't remember that."

"Now," he explained. "We became a team now."

I smiled. "Okay."

He swallowed a sip of water, wiping his mouth with the back of his hand. His eyes drifted away and he stared out the window. At first, I thought he saw something and my breaths quickened, but then his eyes flicked back to mine. "Let's get to know each other."

"Like how?"

"How about we start with this," he began, leaning forward. I swear I thought he was about to kiss me, but instead he smiled and said, "My name is Tristan. Tristan McKinley."

My eyes widened. How did I just then realize that I didn't even know his name? My face grew warm.

"Well?" he asked. "What's yours?"

I blushed. "Skylar Vail."

"Beautiful," he purred, extending his hand toward me. "Nice to meet you, Skylar."

The way he said my name could've made any girl's heart melt, smooth and silky, like liquid milk chocolate.

I took his hand in mine. "Nice to meet you, too, Tristan." He grinned.

I yawned then, pulling my hand back to cover my mouth.

"You know what?" he said, noticing my sleepiness. "It's probably super late. We should go to sleep."

"Why?" I said, mid-yawn. "I was *just* sleeping like half an hour ago."

"But still, we'll need to leave bright and early tomorrow to have enough walking time. You know, to find more life, perhaps. And who knows how often a house like this will appear."

"True. I wonder why it's sitting in the middle of nowhere like this, within all this greenery."

"Who knows," he said. "Nothing in this world makes sense."

"Very true. Did you encounter the cats?"

He smiled, his eyes suddenly bright. "The golden cats? The telepathic cats?"

"Yes!" I nearly screamed. *"This is my city,"* I mocked them.

"You must go," he replied. *"Leave."*

I laughed. "How did you—"

I was interrupted by another screech. Then another. My breaths grew shaky and my bottom lip quivered, my laughter and happiness almost immediately forgotten. Tristan sat up straight, his expression cold and his eyes wide, his body alert like a prairie dog. He stealthily stood up, carefully stepping to the kitchen table to grab the flashlight. I was too afraid to utter his name and call for him but he returned quickly, unharmed, and sat directly beside me, the flashlight at his side.

Another screech.

"Tristan," I whispered. "I'm terrified."

"You're not the only terrified person in this world, you know," he said, mimicking me from earlier, even managing to add a mischievous grin.

"Shut up," I replied, a smile tugging at the corners of my lips. Nevertheless, my body couldn't stop shaking. "We're going to die here."

He wrapped his arm around me. "Shhh," he whispered, his breath warm in my ear. "Just try to relax. Go to sleep."

"Go to sleep? I can't *now*. I... I...." The tears began to flow. "Why is this happening to me? To *us*? What did we do wrong to deserve this?"

"I can think of a few wrongs I did," he said with a short, nearly silent laugh. "But, Skylar, I don't know. I've only been here two days. Just try to relax, okay?"

I cried harder. "I'm so scared. *So* scared. I don't... I just... I miss my mom." I sniffled. "I'm sorry for crying. I don't normally cry in front of others."

"Here, lie down." He adjusted a pillow behind me, and I lay down on my back, staring up at the ceiling as the tears fell from my eyes. The cries from outside continued.

Tristan stood from the couch. "I'll go into the bedroom."

"No," I said sharply. "Stay. Please. Please stay."

"Are you sure?"

"Yes." I swallowed. "I don't want to be alone again."

He nodded, then laid back onto the couch. It was wide enough for us to both lie on comfortably, but one of us had to lie on our side, and that ended up being him.

As we lay there, his eyes closed, mine wide open, I said, "I guess you're not as bad as I thought."

He smiled, his eyes still closed. "You can't say that. You barely know me."

"True. Can you tell me something about yourself?"

"Like what?" I could tell he was sleepy because his voice began to slur.

"What's your favorite color?"

"Blue," he answered. "Yours?"

"Green. Like your eyes."

He smiled again. "I'll take that as a compliment."

"Good," I said. "I meant it as one."

"I like green because it's the color of life."

"I thought your favorite color was blue."

"It is. Blue is the color of the ocean, the water. And I love to swim."

"Technically," I said, "water is clear."

He smiled. "Shut up."

I laughed, closing my eyes.

"Skylar?"

My eyes peeled back open and I looked over to him. His eyes were open, too, his face so close to mine.

"Thanks for tying my jacket around my waist," he told me. "You're right. I probably would've bled out on that road without you." He closed his eyes again. "Good night, team."

I grinned. "Good night, Tristan."

As I lay there, I wondered what Andria would've said if she found out I'd slept on a couch with a boy I barely knew. A boy even more attractive than Zack Corley. I bet she would've freaked out. Big time. But of course she would because who wouldn't?

I closed my eyes again, cuddling closer to Tristan, the screeches echoing in the distance. And when I was sure he was asleep, I gripped his hand and squeezed tightly. But then to my surprise, he squeezed back.

nine

I'd pass by him in the hall and I'd pull my books closer toward my chest, bowing my head. He always looked so handsome, his jet-black, curly hair and his cold yet stunning brown eyes. Every time I saw him, I would have this sick feeling in the pit of my stomach. They said it would get better over time, but sadly it never really did. My happy days grew melancholy as soon as I glanced his way. It's as though for a split second I had forgotten it was over, that he was no longer in my life. As though those days spent staring at Zack Corley across the cafeteria had never occurred, and life was still how it always should have been.

Matt would normally watch me pass, his gaze following my quick strides. I'd walk fast to Andria, never having to say anything because she always knew.

"I know," she'd say, nodding. "I know."

I'd clutch my books harder.

"Matt's not worth it and you know that." I'd shrug. "He's a slug and you're a butterfly, okay? He's slimy and gross, and you're vibrant, beautiful, and free. He's weighing you down, Sky."

"Is it really over?"

She'd nod again, closing her locker. "Yes. Now come on. Time for geometry, your *favorite!*"

I'd look back one more time and he'd be staring at me. *A slug,* I'd think, imagining him as one, which normally made me grin. Then I'd turn back, and Andria and I would walk away.

. . . .

Dr. Richards walks in. I'm still half asleep because Mrs. Carter and I stayed up basically all night. I went on and on about Tristan, and she listened, fascinated. I must've fallen asleep in the middle of my words because I don't remember actually choosing to sleep.

Dr. Richards suddenly begins undoing my straps. I open my mouth to speak but he cuts me off. "One little mishap and these go right back on. Understood?" I nod quickly, grinning. "Okay. Now, be good." He walks away but abruptly stops and turns back to face me. "You seem happier. Are you happier?"

I shrug.

"Well, I hope you are. Being happy is fun." Then he leaves me alone again, my wrists free. I squeal amidst the silence of the room.

. . . .

When I visit Mrs. Carter, she doesn't even appear the least bit tired. In fact, she seems more awake than ever. Her makeup is done beautifully, her dress made of green lace with pink and white flowers.

"Hello, Skylar," she says, overly cheerful with a bright grin. "How are you today?" Her hair is pinned back in a tight, neat bun, the red shimmering. My hair never shimmers like that, too thick and frizzy and curly, so it's usually down and pressed back behind my ears. But hers is the type of red hair I envy—dark like rubies, and soft and thin. Mine is orangey.

I give her a thin smile, lowering my head and strolling to the love seat I sit in every day. "Good," I mumble. "A bit tired."

She laughs, taking a seat as well before crossing her legs and setting a clipboard and some papers in her lap. She presses her pen over her ear. "Me too, actually," she admits. "I'm glad you were about to finally talk about Tristan. I never got the chance to ask, but what made you want to tell me?"

"A dream," I whisper.

"Ah, I figured. I love dreams. They tell us so much about ourselves."

"Really?"

She nods. "Yes. Our latest thoughts, our biggest fears, our wishes, and our passions. They all somehow make their way into our dreams. Perhaps your brain was going crazy because of all the emotions regarding Tristan being locked away so tightly."

I nod, my eyes falling to the floor. "He told me he was looking for me, and that he was close." I glance back up to her

She raises an eyebrow, her eyes wide. "Oh really? Interesting."

"You still don't think he's real, do you?" I mumble.

Mrs. Carter's face falls. "Now, Skylar. I cannot suspect anything just yet, remember? You told me yourself."

"True," I say.

She adjusts herself in the chair, her frail body funny-looking against the wide love seat. "Today, I would like to talk about you. Let's take a break from the... er... place today, okay?"

I press my lips into a line and nod. I'm actually somewhat disappointed.

"Great." She smiles. "Okay, so I would like to do some exercises with you, as I notice you're opening up a bit, which is amazing considering how shortly you've been here."

"What exercises?" I question.

"I desperately want to know how exactly you feel when speaking about the dream, how it has changed you, because I didn't know you before, of course."

"You mean the place?"

She freezes up and then sends me a sour smile. "Yes. My bad."

I pull my knees to my chest, wrapping my arms around them and leaning forward, setting my cheek against a kneecap.

"So, in order to do this certain exercise, I have to get inside your head," she says, adjusting herself in the seat. "We will slowly progress to it by completing smaller exercises."

"Why all these exercises?" I question, my body stiffening. I hate opening up. No matter how much I've happened to "improve," my mind urges to remain silent. And I'm honestly afraid of what I may say. Talking of the happening is one thing; it happened, and I'm telling the story. But speaking my thoughts is a challenge for they are like untamed horses, running freely with no rules and no expectations. They simply do as they please. It will be hard to control them.

"I need to figure out which emotions are keeping you stuck."

"Stuck?" I ask softly, mostly just repeating what she said to see how the word feels on my tongue.

She nods.

"I thought you said I was improving."

"Oh, you are! Of course you are. But you're still not the exact same as you were before this happening. Am I correct?"

I shrug. "I don't even know myself."

She smiles bitterly. "I'm sure you do."

"A bit, I guess." I turn to look at the wall.

"Okay, well, I need you to—Skylar, look at me." I do. "I need you to tell me three things that you are thankful for."

I raise an eyebrow. "What?" She *cannot* be serious.

"I need you to tell me three things that you are thankful for."

I frown. "What the heck is this?"

Mrs. Carter gives me a confused look. "Excuse me?"

I press my lips into a line, pulling my knees closer to my chest.

"Just think, Skylar. Give me three answers, okay? What are you thankful for?" I close my eyes. "Take your time."

I think hard. What am I thankful for? I would say Andria, but she did something terrible, so terrible I wish she hadn't ever been in my life. I would say Mom, but I don't like Mom. Matt is a jerk. Dad left us. Tristan apparently isn't real. I open my eyes slowly, carefully assessing my next words. "I don't know," I finally admit.

"Well, are you thankful for food?" she wonders, her voice soft.

"I don't like eating," I say. "The nurses kind of force me to eat."

"Are you thankful for shelter?"

"I don't really want to be here."

"Are you thankful for being alive?"

I open my lips to speak, but then they slowly shut.

Mrs. Carter sighs. "All right. How about you think about this question and we'll get back to it later, okay?"

"Sure."

"Okay, but Skylar," she begins, leaning forward, "I want you to tell me about yourself."

"Huh?"

"I want to get to know you better." She smiles. "They'll be easy questions, but if you want to skip them, you may. Okay?"

"Okay?" I reply more as a question than a response. I suddenly feel a bit uncomfortable. What exactly does she want to know?

It's not that I dislike Mrs. Carter. In fact, I actually quite like her. She's the most likable person I know at this point in my life. As stated before, she's my current best friend. But my past... there's nothing too great to remember, except the few times with Andria. Everything besides Andria before our downfall seems to be pointless. *Everything* is pointless.

Mrs. Carter's eyes brighten. "Great. Now, what is your favorite animal?"

I smirk. *This'll be easy, I guess.* "Skip."

She grins. "No, not this one."

"What is the point of this?"

"Shhh," she whispers. "Just answer. Relax."

I release my breath. "Fine. A cat."

"Ooo." Her eyebrows rise. "What kind?"

"Just your everyday house cat," I find myself mumbling, sucking in my breath. "I was never allowed to have one in our apartment."

"Aw, that's too bad. What made you want one?"

"My friend Andria had one, and I adored her," I explain, my words coming out quickly. "Tabatha."

"That's a pretty name," Mrs. Carter replies. "And Andria, did she like cats?"

I half-laugh at that, the corners of my lips tugging upwards into a slight smile. "Actually, no. She hates them. She likes dogs but she's allergic. So is her dad."

"You seem to know a lot about Andria."

I nod. "She's my best friend... or was. We sort of got into a fight."

"About what?"

I swallow and shrug, nothing but darkness and jealousy pouring into my mind. "Nothing important."

"Well, obviously it was. She seems to be close, and those relationships only end with something major."

I press my lips together. "It was over a boy. Nothing special. It was just... girl stuff."

"I'm sorry to hear that," she tells me, her expression actually concerned. "Do you miss her?"

"Not as much as I thought I would," I admit.

"And why is that?"

"I don't know. I'm just doing fine without her."

She nods. "Well, that's good. Perhaps it was meant to be, do you think?"

"Why do you say that?"

"Well, I believe everything happens for a reason. But, let's keep this about you." She grins. "What is your favorite food?"

My nose wrinkles at this as I think, images of tasty meals flashing through my head. "Mmmm," I murmur. "Cheeseburgers."

"Oh, my." She laughs. "Those are certainly the best. When was your best memory of cheeseburgers?"

My eyes flash to hers and I notice that she is actually interested, her eyes like liquid and smooth. I lick my lips. "Once when I was like six or seven, my mom and dad took me to this new burger joint down the street. It was my first cheeseburger. It was awesome."

"Sounds lovely. Now, I hear you mention your dad. Was he—"

"I don't want to talk about him," I snap. "Let's talk about cheeseburgers. I only like them with mustard, mayonnaise, and pickles. And cheese, of course."

Mrs. Carter offers a sad smile. "Of course cheese."

We talk, just me and her, about myself for ten minutes or so, my words spilling out like a steady stream, soft and easy. I forget about what I'm even talking about; I just talk, and I feel as though a weight is being lifted from my chest.

Then she takes her pen from behind her ear and asks me, "Now, Sky, how do you feel?"

I pause. "What?"

She grins. "Listen to your feelings. What are they saying?"

I furrow my eyebrows, but then I feel my expression soften, my eyes warming, and I hear it. I actually feel better, happier. I feel lighter.

"Talking about yourself always lightens the mood," she says, smiling.

I bite the inside of my cheek, tasting sweet blood. "I suppose it does," I admit.

"Now, I must ask again, what are three things that you are thankful for?"

I look up to her quickly, my eyes wide. She nods as if to tell me to say it already. She knows I've obtained the answers. She's eager for me to spill.

"For... um... cats," I begin. "And cheeseburgers. And... um..." I trail off, unable to find a third thing.

"What is your favorite color?"

My face goes cold. I had asked Tristan the same question the first night we truly spent together, listening to the cries of those gruesome creatures while lying on the couch. He had said his was blue.

"Green," I answer.

She smiles.

"I'm thankful for the color green... the color of his eyes, and the color of life." And I blush.

"I'm so proud of you, Sky," says Mrs. Carter.

I shrug, grinning. "Now, about the other exercise?"

She nods, tucking her pen behind her left ear again. She folds her hands together, resting her chin on them and staring at me with her gentle yet bold green eyes. They seem to scream out to me; I can hear their piercing whispers within me, and I shudder. I set my feet back onto the floor, sitting up straighter. I can tell she's studying me, figuring me out before she begins. I know that whatever she will say, whatever she will tell me, she will get something out of me that I'm not necessarily ready to share.

I wonder then what the point of all this is, me opening up. I get it; I wasn't the same before, but that isn't exactly a bad thing, right? People change. Whatever happened to me happened for a reason, and it did change me. I don't really know of what sort, but it's evidently shown in my expressions, and in the way I talk. It's as if I had left for the military and the moment I returned I became cold, my fears of the unknown a wall, a barrier around my skin. My feelings are enclosed in a cage that seems to be unwilling to open no matter how hard I try to let my words free from my tongue.

However, perhaps the thoughts will melt away over time and will be forgotten. I know I will never return to the place I had ventured to, despite the voices in my head telling me otherwise, the ones that stop me from comfortably going to sleep. But if I am never going back, I must forget.

So why must I open up? Why must I tell her how I feel? But if I question her of these thoughts, she will manage to find a way to find my inner feelings. I'm afraid of her intense stare but I can't help staring back, biting my bottom lip and twiddling with my thumbs. And I wait.

Her mouth suddenly opens and she speaks softly, "Skylar, I want you to close your eyes." I do so gently. "Good. I want you to imagine yourself as a young girl, at the age of five or six. You are in the park with your parents. You are happy, and the atmosphere is blissful. You twirl about the grass in a bright sundress, and...."

. . . .

I am young, frail. I dance about the park, giggling and squealing. My parents watch from the bench, Dad's arms wrapped around Mom. She actually looks happy, and young. Her wrinkles are gone and she's wearing clothes that finally fit. Her hair isn't as gray, and her skin isn't as yellow. For once, in what seems like centuries, my mother isn't decaying before my very eyes.

Dad looks just as I remember him last: tall, handsome, with dark hair and a scruffy beard. He looks happy, as he always did, a goofy smile plastered across his face. He wears a nice, neat outfit, as if he had just came back from church.

"Come here, Sky," my father calls. I skip over to the bench and sit beside my parents, my feet dangling off the side. I lean back against my dad as he plays with my hair. "Look at the clouds. What do you see?"

I look up and see a bunny rabbit on a bicycle. Then I see a cat chasing a mouse. Then a dragon breathing fire. I smile as I stare at the clouds, the sun warm on my cheeks.

But all of a sudden, my surroundings go dark, as if someone has flicked off the light switch. I am also older now, my skin wrinkled and my fingers bony. My body aches and my throat is raw. I look around, but all I see is darkness. I breathe in and the bitter air stings my lungs. I can hardly breathe. I call for my parents but I cannot speak. And my feet don't move. It's like that dream I had where Tristan came to visit me; I can't do anything for it's as if I'm not even there.

Then a light appears. I see my dad. He's yelling at Mom. She's crying at the kitchen table, her head in her hands. Dad has a backpack on, filled with some clothes and a few books. He's leaving, and Mom isn't stopping him.

I see myself standing in the doorway of my bedroom. I am eleven, my wild morning hair sticking up in messy clumps. My eyes are wide and my face reveals how terrified I am. I attempt to call out to myself. "Stop him!" I try to say. "Don't let him leave us again!" But the words don't manage to escape. I can't even close my eyes. I'm forced to watch, trapped in this old body that isn't mine.

Dad walks right out the door, slamming it behind him. Mom is screaming. I can feel her pain. And I still stand in the doorway, my mouth open and my eyes glazed over. I was confused. I can remember the feeling. I figured Dad would come back later. He couldn't leave forever, right?

But I was wrong.

That's when the light dims again and I'm alone in the room, nothing but the sound of my shivering breaths and my beating heart echoing among the nothingness.

. . . .

I open my eyes, gasping for breath. Mrs. Carter grasps my shoulders tightly. "Shhh," she says. "It's okay. You did so well. You're back. It's okay."

"What happened?" I ask, shocked, unable to recall a certain thing.

Instead of answering, she hugs me. "You did *so* well."

"But what—"

"I think you're ready to start group sessions."

"What?"

"Group sessions. Of course, we'll have individual ones, but we can—"

"There's more?"

Mrs. Carter slowly pulls away, her soft eyes studying me carefully.

"There's more like me?"

She smiles. "Of *course*, Sky! We'll meet them tomorrow. I think you'll like them."

I breathe in and breathe out, deeply, steadily. "Did I really do well?"

"Yes. You did great."

I can still feel the cold air hanging in my lungs, yet I don't remember anything but darkness. Maybe that's all it was. But my clouded mind can't think clearly and my body is still tight, so I don't know for sure. By the looks of it, I doubt I ever will.

ten

My mother is an unkind woman. At least for the last few years, anyway. Before Dad left us she was generous and kind, but now she is cold, all her happiness drained away and her insides filled with muck, her heart replaced with an ice cube. She wears big clothes, her hair pulled back into a messy ponytail, and no makeup, the bags under her eyes visible from miles away. She's lost weight, as well as friends. My father's departure destroyed her.

She works at a restaurant about a block away, struggling to pay the bills in time by working extra hours and night shifts, so in other words, she's never home. She works every day, or so she says. Once, I was out with Andria and we saw her at the bar with some girls I had never seen before. Ever since that day, I've wondered if she really works at all. But I shouldn't complain for the lack of food and furniture because if I were to, she'd make me get a job, too.

I know she went through a lot when my dad left us for his hot twenty-year-old intern and moved to Georgia with her, but that was still five years ago. I get that I wasn't romantically in love with my dad like she was, but he *was* my dad, and I've had to get over him, too. I spent two years depressed, staring at our front door and hoping for his return, calling him constantly. He was my hero. He was my dad. And now he doesn't even wish me happy birthday. I also overheard my mom on the phone one day with her friend, saying she "can't believe that pig already has two children." I just guessed the pig was my dad.

When I broke up with Matt, my mother didn't even care. She looked me in the eye and said, "Get over it. He left you. He's not coming back." And walked away. That's the most my mom has ever said to me at once in the last five years. Well, I suppose that's an exaggeration, but still.

Yes, I wish I had a different mother, but oh well. I guess I didn't have the best luck, but that's just life.

Andria told me she's just hard on me because I have my dad's eyes, as well as his personality—reserved yet open-minded with sharp wit. But I doubt that. I just think she's jealous that I'm over him. I don't usually think of him often, but he's all she talks about, even now.

I sometimes lie awake at night and pray for Mom, even though we never go to church besides that one time for Easter. Andria is religious, and she gives me Bible verses a lot to reflect on. I do say I believe in God, or at least in a higher power however, for some things I pray about and wish for actually appear. Everything except for Dad returning. And Mom getting better. By now, I've agreed that Mom is unfixable. She's broken, as broken as a shattered vase.

. . . .

The next day, a nurse, Samantha, enters my room a few hours after breakfast to take me to Mrs. Carter's office. I'm nervous because this is my first day of group sessions and I'm certain I'll hate it. I haven't seen another person my age since the day before I came here, which was about a week ago.

I also look like crap. I haven't brushed my hair in two days, have only taken about three showers since I arrived here because I was forced to by a nurse—they force me to do a lot—and I'm wearing a big, white T-shirt and some blue shorts, which the facility gave me. My blue eyes are more clear than blue, and my body is thin and my skin is sickly. Or in other words, I basically look like I've been to hell and back, and I doubt anyone else looks as frightening.

But I am entirely mistaken.

I walk in to see three girls and two boys, wearing similar outfits with similar hair and similar long faces, all staring at me as if I have suddenly grown an extra nose, their eyebrows furrowed in curiosity.

"Hey, Skylar," Mrs. Carter says happily. Today her hair is down and flattened, and she wears jeans with a red blouse. "Please, take a seat."

I sit between a boy with a square face and black hair, and a girl who is so skinny she sort of looks like a skeleton. The boy resembles Matt in a way as he gapes at me with widened, crystal blue eyes. And the girl beside me has dirty blonde hair and charcoal eyes, which hold a world of despair within them. I feel like I look better than all of them, which surprises me greatly.

"Everyone," Mrs. Carter begins, "I would like you all to stand up one by one and introduce yourself. Say your name, your age, something cool about you, and your reason for being here." She nods to the boy on the far left. "Caleb, how about you start?"

The boy stands. He has messy brown hair and sharp brown eyes. He looks directly at me, which forces me to quickly glance away. His stare stabs me like a knife. "My name is Caleb," he murmurs in a voice much too deep for himself. "I am seventeen. I am, or *was*, on the varsity swim team for my school, so yeah, I like to swim. And I have pain disorder, which led to severe anxiety and depression."

"Thank you, Caleb."

Next, the boy beside me stands. He is much taller than I thought, at least six-foot. "My name is David. I am fifteen." He swallows, swaying back and forth. "I like to draw sometimes. And, uh, I'm depressed and suicidal because my mother abused me growing up." He sits down.

I gulp; it's my turn. I carefully stand, folding my arms in front of my chest. I look at Mrs. Carter and Mrs. Carter only. "My name is Skylar," I say. "I'm sixteen. I… um… like to read, I guess. And I…." I pause and look around the room, catching the frozen stares. "I went to a weird place in my sleep, and I guess it made me go crazy or something." And I sit down.

"So, like a *dream*?" some snobby girl with jet-black hair and a thin face asks me, leaning forward. "What kind of crap is that?"

I raise an eyebrow and stare her straight in the eyes. Her blue eyes, colder than mine, are filled with wildness, like roaring rapids splashing around her dilated pupils. I can sense the heat within her, boiling beneath her skin. "*Excuse* me?" I ask bluntly.

"Onyx," Mrs. Carter snaps. "That is not necessary. What did I tell you before Skylar came in?"

"*Onyx*?" I laugh. "What kind of name is that?"

"*Skylar*," Mrs. Carter hisses.

"The name of a powerful black stone," Onyx grits out. "*Duh*, dream girl."

"Onyx," Mrs. Carter says, pronouncing her name slowly and bitterly, as though it stings her tongue. "Do you believe that your reason for being here is superior to Skylar's?"

"As a matter of fact," she says with a smirk, "I do."

"Then you should share next." Mrs. Carter's eyes are hard.

All curious eyes turn to Onyx, wide and astonished as she stands. She's at least five-foot-eight, which happens to be tall compared to my five-foot-three self. She looks directly at me and runs a hand through her tangled yet luscious black locks. She's not as thin as I, or the other girls. In fact, she actually looks healthy and strong. "My name is Onyx... ever since I was seven, at least. I am seventeen. The only hobby I have is staying alive. And my reason for being here is because I have post-traumatic stress disorder. Not because I was in the military." She laughs at that, but then her face grows serious as she looks at me sternly. "But because I was raped for five years by my own freaking father, and my mother didn't believe me."

She sucks in her breath, looking to me. "Try that on for size. You think having a dream is such a big deal that you have to come *here* to live with the so-called *freaks*?" She shakes her head. "I have nightmares every freaking night. Of my own dang father. Of him using me. *Every* night. So don't you *ever*—"

"*Onyx*," Mrs. Carter snaps. "That's *enough*."

Onyx turns to look at her and frowns before she quickly sits. "Whatever," she says, pressing her face into her hands.

I look to the floor.

"Carol." Mrs. Carter sighs with a thin smile, tucking a strand of hair behind her ear. "Go next, would you?"

The girl beside me stands. "My name is Carol," she says carefully. "I'm fourteen. I like to play soccer. Or I used to. And I have anorexia." This was pretty evident since her legs were about a couple inches wide, her face so thin I wanted to cringe.

The last girl stands once Carol sits. She's the only one here with warm brown skin, and she has unnatural, short red hair which sits on her shoulders in a frizzy mess.

She's thin, too, but not as thin as Carol. And she's actually quite beautiful. More beautiful than all the other girls. "I'm Jordan. I'm fifteen. I liked to hang out with my friends and my boyfriend. That's all I really did until I got sick. I have depression."

I can't quite pay attention to Jordan very much, for Onyx's glare distracts me.

"Thank you for sharing, everyone," Mrs. Carter says to us. "Now, how about we talk about how we've been, and how we are feeling today."

. . . .

Apparently I have to eat lunch with them now, which is right after the group sessions. Carol and Caleb walk with me to the cafeteria.

"Don't worry about Onyx," Caleb tells me, obviously noticing my tight stare on the girl's back as she walks quickly ahead of us. But once he says this, I tear my eyes from her and look at him. "She's only been here three weeks. She's not doing so well yet."

"Then why is she in group sessions?" I ask quietly, glancing down to the floor.

"Because she's been here for three weeks already," Carol tells me. "And I don't know if you've noticed but none of us are doing too well. That's why we're here." I look at her and she smiles sheepishly. "But don't worry. Everyone gets better." Her voice is so thin I feel like I could crack it by squeezing the air as she speaks.

"She's just tough," Caleb says. "Don't let her get to you."

"I wasn't letting her get to me," I mumble. Then I look at him again. "What is pain disorder?"

"Huh?"

"What you have."

He laughs nervously.

"You'll figure it out soon enough," Carol tells me.

"It's gotten better," Caleb says, his voice harsh, the trace of his recent laughter suddenly gone.

Carol's eyes widen at his words and she lowers her head.

"I think we're *all* wondering how a dream can make a person go crazy, though," Caleb says, but for some reason, I don't realize he's talking to me at first. "Skylar?" he asks, clearing his throat. My eyes meet his. "How did a *dream* make you go crazy?"

"You don't believe me?"

"Huh? No, I do. I never said I didn't."

"Then you wouldn't be asking."

"Skylar, I'm asking because it's interesting."

"Mmmhm," I reply, looking to the floor.

"Much more interesting than any of our illnesses."

"You talk too much," I say coldly.

Caleb doesn't respond. As we continue to the cafeteria, I look to my right and see David and Jordan talking and laughing away, an evident spark between them, which is odd because I could've sworn that she said she had a boyfriend.

Once we make it to the cafeteria, I feel the doctors and other patients eye me carefully. I wonder if they know what I did to Amelia, or if it's just because I am new. I swallow, glancing at the ground.

The great thing about going to the cafeteria is I can pick out my own food. No more having to eat PB&Js and chicken nuggets when I'm in the mood for Mexican. But it's crowded and I feel entirely exposed, as though I'm naked. I haven't been around this many people in a while.

"You okay?" Caleb whispers to me. "You look sick."

I swallow and nod. "I'm fine."

We get in line with our trays. I reach for a spoon and pile some mac-n-cheese on my plate. Then some carrots. Some rice. A roll. Some honeydew. A very odd combination. As I stare at my plate I think back to the first few days I was here, when I wouldn't eat a thing. Now I realize how starved I truly am. Does that mean I'm healing, or that I'm just hungry?

I grab a Coke and head to the table with Caleb and Carol. Jordan and David are already there. So is Onyx, but she sits toward the end by herself, gnawing on an apple.

Caleb, Carol, and I sit across from Jordan and David as we eat. Everyone else talks but I sit silently, my eyes drifting across the other people in the cafeteria. I wonder why they are here and try to figure out their backgrounds. Are they doctors, are they mentally ill, or are they just normal people?

"Never seen a big crowd before, dream-girl?" Onyx asks me from across the table, laughing. I look at her and she smirks, slowly biting into her apple. All heads turn her way.

"Shut up, Onyx," Caleb tells her.

"What?" she asks, her mouth full of apple. "I'm just making conversation."

I roll my eyes and turn away.

"Well, yeah," Onyx says. "Welcome to the home of the freaks. This is it. This is where you belong." My eyes dart to meet hers. "Dreams are pretty scary, aren't they?"

"Why do you hate me?" I snap, my eyebrows furrowed.

"*Me?*" she gasps. "*Hate?* I would never do such a thing. Hating is for *wimps*." She bites into her apple again, even though it is almost gone.

I look at everybody else and notice how they look uncomfortable, pressing their lips into lines and bowing their heads.

"Listen," I start, "I'm not in the mood. I don't know if you want to keep peace or not but *I* do. I'm not in the mood for any stupid games."

"You're not in the *mood?*" she asks. "Oops, my bad."

I frown. "Can't you just leave me alone?"

"Sorry, but no can do. We're roommates now, you know." She sighs. "What fun."

My mouth falls open. "Wh-*what*?"

She smiles and then stands. Apparently all she ate was an apple. "Yep. I'll see you tomorrow, dream-girl. Don't dream too hard tonight." Then she laughs and walks away, her long black hair waving behind her. On her way out, she throws her apple into the trash so violently the can nearly tips over.

. . . .

"I am *not* sleeping in the same room as that… *thing*," I snap at Mrs. Carter. "I *swear* she wants to kill me."

Mrs. Carter offers me a sad look. "She's not all that bad, Skylar. Post-traumatic stress can change people."

"She calls herself Onyx, for crying out loud." I sigh. "She's going to *kill* me."

"No, she's not."

"Why do I even *need* a roommate?" I throw my arms into the air and then massage my forehead with my thumb and index finger, closing my eyes and breathing in deep.

"Being isolated for too long can increase your illness," says Mrs. Carter. "Once Dr. Richards was sure you were better, he agreed that you need a roommate in order to interact with others and bond with them."

I gaze up at her, my eyes cold. "I was doing just fine on my own."

Mrs. Carter grins, shaking her head slowly. "Give it a week and if you change your mind, you can let me know. I think you two will really like each other."

"I doubt it." I sigh.

She laughs. "Just give it a week, okay? She'll move into your room tomorrow afternoon after our session."

I close my eyes again.

"So, Sky, are you ready to talk about what happened some more?"

eleven

I woke up slowly. The screeches had vanished, and the realization sent a feeling of relief through my stiff body. I opened my eyes, the early-morning sunlight from the nearby windows leaking through and melting over my body, covering me like a blanket. I rolled over to my side to wake Tristan, but my stomach plummeted when I saw he wasn't there. I sat up quickly, my breaths sharp and short. Had he left without me again? He *couldn't* have!

I stood from the couch, running my hands through my messy hair, which had fallen from its ponytail overnight. I remembered when he said he wanted to wake up early to get a good start on the journey ahead, but why would he tell me that if he was just going to leave without me?

I ran all over the house calling his name, but he was nowhere to be found. I began to cry. I couldn't believe he had left me *again*.

I slowly made my way to the front door while shaking my head, tears streaming down my cheeks as I cursed under my breath. I opened the door and stepped outside, the crisp morning breeze gently blowing against my puffy face. I gazed out at the endless horizon, the familiar green sight from yesterday. I was trying to figure out where he had gone. He was probably miles away by then.

"Good morning."

I screamed, jumping into the air and grasping my chest. I looked to my left to see Tristan, his green eyes wide. "You okay?" He was sitting cross-legged on the grass, holding a white cup with orange juice inside. I stared at him blankly, my heartbeat racing beneath my chest so fast it hurt. His dark brown hair was blown back by the breeze, his expression buzzing with concern.

I frowned then, very much relieved but also angry. I kicked my boot at the ground, spraying him with grass and dirt.

"*Hey*!" he spat, gritting his teeth. "What's your problem?"

"I thought you *left* me!" I shouted back just as harshly. "You jerk! You scared me!"

He set down the cup and ran his fingers through his hair, knocking the dirt bits out of the messy locks. "I told you I wouldn't leave," he said while looking up at me, his eyes misty. "I said we're a team, right? My bad for letting you sleep."

I looked out to the horizon again, feeling bad. My face softened as I glanced back to him, pressing my lips into a line. "Sorry," I said flatly, my voice still drenched in sadness, my eyes puffy and red.

He smirked, shaking his head. "Sit down."

I did, crossing my legs, too. We stared out at the horizon together, watching the egg-yolk sun rise slowly.

"Would you really miss me if I left?" he asked.

"Shut up," I said, trying to hide my blush by turning my head. My stomach growled.

"Let's get breakfast," he stated, standing up. "Then we'll head out."

"Why don't we just stay here?" I asked, standing up with him.

"We won't find anything if we just stay here," he told me, looking at me with those bright, beautiful eyes. "Come on. We should hurry."

And I followed him into the house.

. . . .

I had some orange juice myself, along with a granola bar. We had eaten the entire box of Cheez-It's the night before, and so all that remained were a few more granola bars, one more oatmeal cream pie, and some expired bags of fruit snacks. Tristan and I took what we could find of those seldom choices, and then I finally realized I didn't have a backpack to put any of it into. Tristan laughed when I asked him where mine was and fetched it from a bottom cabinet, tossing it over. "Your music taste is pretty outdated," he told me.

"Whatever," I said, finding my phone inside and clutching it tightly, a satisfying warmth spreading throughout my veins. I pulled it out and turned it on; there was only forty percent left. "Thanks for using all of my battery," I snarled, glaring at him and dropping the phone back into the bag.

He laughed. "It was at fifty-six percent when I found it." He raised his shirt then and my stomach plummeted and my eyes quickly flicked away, as if I had never seen a bare chest before. "Can you redo this for me?"

I cautiously gazed back to him. The shirt he had around his wound had been bled through, the blood now a dark brown color and crusted over his chest. It wasn't completely finished bleeding, but at least it wasn't by much. I nodded, then walked over to him, finally realizing just how tall he was. I'm a short person, so perhaps he wasn't *that* tall—probably five-nine or so—but I still felt weak beside him, as though he could tap me on the shoulder and I'd fly away. I bit my lip as I gently touched his hip, peeling back the shirt from the wound. It already looked better from the day before.

We didn't have much time since it was nearly seven in the morning and we should've left at six, so I worked fast. I grabbed a different shirt and fetched more alcohol. "Does it hurt?" I asked him when I was finished, dropping some extra shirts and the alcohol into my backpack.

"No," he wheezed out through gritted teeth. "Not at all."

"You don't have to look tough for me, you know," I told him, slinging my bag onto my right shoulder and redoing my hair, tossing it into a disastrous bun.

"What?"

"You don't have to impress me." I slipped on the other strap and tightened the bag so it sat sturdy on my shoulders.

He smirked, following me to the door after picking up the flashlight from the table. "Don't worry, I'm not trying to. I'm just naturally a tough guy."

"I can tell," I replied with a grin.

"But is it working?"

"Is what working?"

"The tough-guy-ness. Is it winning you over?"

I looked at him, an eyebrow arched. "Pfft, you wish."

"Ouch."

We walked out the front door, the chilly morning air once again grazing over my skin. I folded my arms across my chest, waiting for Tristan to step in front and lead the way. I'll admit that I was very dependent on him for whatever reason.

"What happens if we don't find a house again?" I asked him quietly, staring out into the openness.

He looked at me kindly, but his expression was subconsciously drenched in fear. "Then we're screwed." He nodded to the left, grinning. "Ready?"

We strolled out into the nothingness, the never-ending green, upon the very same road as yesterday. Tristan and I didn't speak much for a while, but I could feel him glancing my way continuously, as though he were making sure I hadn't left his side. Whenever his eyes scanned my body, I stiffened, my insides growing warm. I felt entirely exposed. Is it weird that I tried to avoid his gaze? Of course, I had never stood that close to an attractive guy before, and I was petrified—which was ironic because I had slept beside him the night before and was perfectly fine. But that was also under different circumstances, I supposed.

Eventually, he said, "Tell me about yourself, Skylar."

I looked at him then, finally, and couldn't help but laugh. He sounded just like a counselor. Also ironic.

"What?" he questioned, smiling yet confused.

"Nothing." I giggled, trying to wipe away my grin with my palm. When I had calmed down, I asked, "What do you want to know?"

He shrugged, smirking. "Anything. I'm bored as heck."

I laughed again, but not as hard. "You're *bored*? In this place?"

He nodded. "Yeah, this place is pretty boring, don't you think? Everybody gone, the giant cats--*Totally* boring."

I sighed. "Of course."

"But seriously, tell me something. Anything."

"There's nothing that interesting about me," I replied quickly, looking ahead.

"Sure there is."

I swallowed, the corners of my lips tugging upwards. "I like to read."

"See? That's a start," he told me. "What do you like to read?"

Images of all of my favorite books flashed in my mind, and I realized then how much I had missed home. And Mom, even. And Andria. I felt sick. Why was I happy, having fun, when Mom and Andria were back home, probably looking for me and scared sick? I shouldn't have been happy. I shouldn't have been laughing.

"Let's stop talking, please," I mumbled, my tone growing cold.

"Wha—"

"*Please.*"

"Okay, okay," he spat defensively. We walked in silence for minute or so when he asked, "Can we at least listen to music?"

I looked at him, raising an eyebrow.

"You actually do have a pretty good taste in music," he said, smiling bitterly.

I rolled my eyes, a smile of my own forcing its way through. I reached into my bag and took out my phone and headphones. We each put in a bud and "Say It Ain't So" by Weezer began to play vibrantly into our ears, our steps quickening to match the beat. I glanced over at him and saw that his eyes were closed as he listened, his mind somewhere else. I sighed, grinning before turning back ahead.

Maybe it is okay to have fun. Because I figured, there's really no use in being sad.

But suddenly, Tristan's eyes widened and he moaned out in pain, grasping his wound. The earbuds fell from our ears, right in the middle of "My Name Is Jonas." "Oh my gosh!" I screamed, grabbing his shoulder to help him balance as his suddenly limp body swayed. "What happened?"

His breaths were heavy and he carefully stood upright once more, his stare distant. "I'm fine," he mumbled.

"Obviously *not*," I cried, gritting my teeth. "We should stop and take a little break."

"No," he spat. "We can't. We gotta keep moving." He pressed his lips into a firm line to lock in the pain.

"Tristan—"

"I'm *fine*," he said harshly, as if he were reassuring himself that he was okay, rather than saying it to me. He looked at me then, his eyes hard, the cloudiness gone, and replaced with fear. "I'm *fine*."

"Okay," I whispered as we continued walking. Tristan didn't utter another word, the atmosphere between us strangely thick, the air hard to breathe.

. . . .

The day dragged on without Tristan talking. Of course, I first told him to shut his lips, but nobody really *means* it. Not for forever, anyway.

Eventually Tristan and I spotted a hole in the ground that led into an opened cave once the sun began to set. It was the first unique thing I had seen the entire day really, that hole. "You think this will be secure enough?" I wondered to the cold Tristan, who didn't even look my way.

"It's fine," he said bitterly. "I'll make a fire."

Once we cautiously walked down into the hole and I'd slung my backpack from my shoulders and let it fall to the floor, I sighed. "*Everything* is fine, apparently."

Tristan shot me a quick glance, then knelt on the floor to find rocks, wincing.

"You know how to make fire?" I asked, watching him rub two black rocks together, creating a sound that made each of us cringe. Tristan only nodded in reply, his eyes focused on the rocks and the rocks only, as if I weren't even present in the cave with him. "Are you going to talk at all?" Nothing. "Say something!"

"Something," he muttered.

I sighed, sitting on the ground. The cave was certainly not as fascinating as the house, but it definitely could do for the night. Or I hoped it could, for I wasn't really certain, and I doubt Tristan was, either. And I was nervous because the night creatures could easily find us there. They hated light and Tristan was evidently making fire to stop them from coming in, but we still weren't completely sure it would work.

I silently watched Tristan work to calm my crazed thoughts. I wanted to listen to music, but my phone was sadly at 23 percent and I wanted to save the battery.

I wondered to myself then: Why us? As I watched Tristan make the fire, the sparks flying from the rocks, I wondered why *we* had ventured here in our sleep. Why everyone else had remained safe on Earth, and we had disappeared to this place during the night. I wanted to ask Tristan this question, but 1) I doubted he had a good answer, or an answer at all, and 2) I also doubted he'd make an effort to tell me whatever words came to mind because 3) he wasn't speaking to me.

At last, a flame started within the small bush of grass Tristan had brought down with us. It was subtle but the warmth was soothing, even so distant from it. "Yay!" I exclaimed, smiling. Tristan glanced up at me, the firelight reflecting in his eyes, yet his expression was colorless besides that. His stare sent butterflies through my body. I smiled even bigger. "Good job. How'd you learn to do that?"

He sighed, sitting against the wall and looking up to the low ceiling. "I thought *you* were the cold one," he mumbled. "Why are you being all chirpy now?"

"I'm not cold," I said. "In fact, I think I'm actually quite nice."

"*Sure.*"

"I fixed your wound. A little."

His eyes flicked to mine, his head still raised.

"That reminds me," I began, picking at the loose skin around my finger nails. "I should look at your wound again."

"Can we stop talking?" he snapped, yet somewhat mimicking my voice.

"But it needs to be—"

"*No*. Stop reminding me of it."

I frowned as he looked back up to the ceiling. I stared at the fire as I gritted my teeth.

"I like to read all sorts of books," I uttered quietly. I felt Tristan's eyes quickly flick to me. "Especially romance. But I also like basically *every* genre. My favorite book is science fiction, *Ender's Game*."

"I thought I asked if we could stop talking," Tristan said coldly.

I looked at him. "Oh yes, you did. I'm just talking to myself, not to you. But you're welcome to listen if you want." I glanced back at the fire and couldn't help but grin. Tristan didn't reply, so I continued. "I don't read as much as it may seem, though. I read occasionally, whenever I'm not watching TV. But I don't want to say I like TV as a hobby, or as an interesting thing about me, you know? TV is boring. Most everyone likes TV, but only a few people like to read. People with open minds like to read, which I've been known to have. Apparently it's evident I read because my head is always up in the clouds, and I'm always thinking about unrealistic worlds and scenarios."

I laughed. Once it subsided, I breathed in deeply "Gosh, I do that *way* too much. But anyway, I do like to read. I like TV more, but I don't tell people that." I turned from the fire and stared deep into Tristan's eyes.

He watched me with so much intensity that anyone normal would quickly glance away, as if looking into his eyes was forbidden. But I continued to stare for some reason, and the corners of my lips tugged upwards into a friendly smile. He just looked at me, studying me with a straight, empty face. "Did you decide to listen?" I wondered.

He nodded, closing his eyes. "Keep talking."

So I did. "I have one true friend. Or I guess I *did* have one true friend. We sort of got into a fight over a boy."

"Oh? A boy, you say?" Tristan butted in. I turned to him and saw that he wore a subtle sneer, his eyes appearing more alive.

I grinned. "*Yes*, a boy." I turned back to the fire, watching the red and orange tails dance in the air. "Anyway, I suppose we're no longer friends, so I'm kind of afraid that when…*if* I return, I won't have anybody."

"Tell me about this guy."

I glanced at Tristan, furrowing my eyebrows. "He's not important. Just an ex."

"How did y'all meet? What happened?"

I breathed in deeply. "Okay, well, once upon a time, there was this guy named Matt. I never really noticed him, until one day one of his friends walked over to me and said, 'hey, my buddy Matt thinks you're cute' and then he gave me his number on a note. I stared up to Matt. He stared back at me, his face as red as a tomato. I wasn't really sure if I wanted to text him, but that same night I ended up messaging him anyways out of excitement, and for the next month or so we texted every night until about two in the morning. He was remarkable. He was amazing. He was the kindest guy I had ever met."

I closed my eyes, breathing out. "Then we started dating. We were together for seven months. That's a pretty long time for a high school couple. But I was blind, apparently, because he treated me like crap the entire time, and I never noticed it until this one day when he didn't answer his phone all night, and I found out he went to a party the night before. You know, one with alcohol and drugs and girls."

I opened my eyes, wiping away the newly formed tears with my index finger. I watched the fire before speaking again. "I couldn't believe it. But then I went back through all the memories. There was more bad than good. He made fun of me, flirted with other girls in front of me, called me names. I was always the one to make plans. He rarely texted me back because he was playing video games. The entire time he had made me feel like crap, and I hadn't even noticed because it was my first relationship. I didn't know any better! My mom didn't care, and my friend wasn't there for me during our relationship because apparently, she had been the reason he treated me like crap. They had a thing behind my back the entire time and didn't care to tell me."

Tears began to fall faster, my chest filling with an uncomfortably hot ache. "I thought long and hard about everything he did before I broke up with him. Before I even said anything to him, I couldn't get out of bed for three days. I was so heartbroken."

I swallowed. *Am I really saying this?* But I continued anyway, despite my embarrassment. "It's been about three months since we've been apart. *Three months.* That's a quarter of an entire year! You'd think I'd be over it by now, but every day is exactly the same. It always has been. I still wake up and want to die because I miss him. I miss him so much. You'd think I'd be over it, right? You'd think I would be. But with him dating my once best friend now and me left with no one, my own mother telling me to grow up, to get over it as if it's as easy as breathing, and seeing him laugh, being fine without me... it hurts. It hurts so much. I feel so abandoned. And alone. And betrayed, and—"

"*Skylar*," Tristan snapped.

I turned to him quickly. "What?"

He gave me a sincere smile.

I realized then that I had been bawling, tears streaming down my face.

"I'm sorry," I mumbled, wiping away my tears. My face grew red. I was never a crier, yet by that point, I had already lost it twice—no, technically *three* times—in front of him. Why was I always crying? Was it normal to cry? Perhaps it was in this place.

Tristan shook his head. "No, Sky. It's okay. Don't be embarrassed."

But I broke down again, sobbing and pressing my face into my hands. Seconds later, I felt Tristan at my side, his arm around me and pulling me to him. "Shhh," he whispered in my ear. "It's okay. Just cry. Let it out."

"Tristan," I breathed out, looking up at him with wet eyes. He met my gaze. "Why is it that I'm still crying over him? Why am I still hurting when he's doing fine? He's happy, and I'm here in this scary world with giant cats." We both found ourselves laughing at that.

"Well, Sky," Tristan muttered, pulling me closer, "sometimes you will feel like dying, and you will feel like giving up. But you know what?"

I swallowed, wiping my tears again. "What?"

"That's just life. That's growing up. You may lose people, and you may go through things nobody in life should, but that's just life. And at the end of each day, you just have to remember that it's only a day."

I grinned. "You always know exactly what to say."

He smiled a close-mouthed smile, his eyes warm, comforting. I stared up into them, swallowing.

"I know what will make you feel better," he said calmly.

"What?" I asked, biting my lip.

He reached for the bag then. "Food," he laughed.

I smiled. "The ticket to any girl's heart."

He set the bag between us as my stomach growled. I kept forgetting how hungry I was in that world. I guess because there's was so much occurring, food was the last on my mind.

We each split the only oatmeal cream pie and each took a granola bar and a bag of fruit snacks, eating silently. And that sliced through the moment. His grasp on me loosened and we sat without speaking for a bit, the bright firelight flickering among the suffocating space of the cave. A strange comfort crept over me while I sat with him, and not just because he was insanely attractive and cared for me in a way that literally nobody else did. It was as though we had been friends for centuries. Like that moment was normal: sitting by the fire with him, eating snacks in a vacant cave in a vacant world. It wasn't supposed to be anyone else, either. It was supposed to be him sitting beside me. I knew that.

And it helped to let out the emotions, because my sadness was then a memory. I remembered Andria holding me, soothing me, helping me let it out. She'd tell me to cry because crying helps. I'd hold on tighter, and her silence would grow thicker as my sobs overtook her voice.

Suddenly, the screeches began from outside again and we each stiffened, slowly finding our bodies drift apart, our eyes gazing out to the opening of the cave. I wasn't sure if the fire would completely keep us safe, but I knew Tristan was sure, for he settled down after a few moments of being perched up like a prairie dog. "I'm never going to get used to them," Tristan mumbled.

"And you think I will?" I asked, grinning. The tears were stained on my face, yet the feeling of despair was no longer lingering within.

The screeches grew nearer and nearer, but the creatures never seemed to venture as near as the opening of our cave, and they certainly never came in. Eventually, after a few minutes of listening to their howls, I began trying to understand what exactly they were. Were they just like us, or aliens? Were they mad, or simply hungry? I wondered if Tristan and I would eventually end up like them. And why the light? Why did they only thrive in darkness?

But there were so many unanswered questions about that world; I doubted figuring out what the creatures were would happen anytime soon. I still had no idea where I was.

"Thank you for talking about Matt," Tristan yawned as he lay on the floor, stretching out across the rock. He stared up at the ceiling. "I'm sorry I was mad."

I bit my lip, looking at him. "It's okay. I don't blame you."

His eyes flicked to mine. They were sad. "I suppose it'd only be fair if you knew a little about me, then." He stared back up to the ceiling.

I lay down on the ground beside him. It was terribly uncomfortable and cold. I watched the flickering shadow of the firelight dance upon the ceiling. The figures looked like two people twirling about each other, playing tag.

"I suppose it'd be fair, yes," I whispered, my thin voice slicing through the near-silent air. Of course, besides the crackling fire and the cries from outside it was near-silent. But at that moment as I lay beside Tristan, all the other noise slowly bled away until nothing but our soft voices and my quick heartbeat was heard. We both turned to each other, staring into one another's eyes. By instinct, I quickly turned away.

"All right," he began, his voice unusually cold. He inhaled a deep breath, turning back to face the ceiling. "I am—or *was*—a very bad kid. I was rebellious. I snuck out, went to parties, hooked up with random girls, drank alcohol, smoked weed. I used to do *all* that bad stuff. I mean, even before I got here I did stuff like that. I just wasn't as bad. I was an *awful* kid. I don't even know why I did it. To be cool, I guess? I don't know. But my parents sent me away when I was thirteen to live with my grandmother in Ohio. But then I was *so* awful; I wasn't even fourteen when my grandmother sent me back." I hear Tristan chuckling to himself at that. "But anyway, long story short is I went to a juvenile prep school in New York City. It's one of those rich, bad schools. Like, you know, you go there when you're bad, and it's for rich kids. 'Cause my parents are, like, really rich. I'm rich. Anyway, I've stayed there for the last two years. It's helped a bit, I guess, but I'm still not a good guy."

It doesn't make any sense. I turn to look at him. He looks at me, too. "You're good to me, though."

"Well, yeah," he says. "There's no use in being mean to you because you're literally the last person on Earth besides me."

I stared at him. He stared at me, licked his lips.

"Why are you bad?" I asked him.

He shrugged. "I don't like being reminded of it but it's just who I am, I guess. I just thank God I'm not in jail. Thankfully, I'm not *that* bad." He smirked.

"You believe in God?"

"Sort of, kind of. More so than not."

"What? Why? If you're a bad guy, how can you believe in God?"

"So," he said with a grin, "I'm guessing you're not religious?"

I shrugged, turning to face the dancing shadows again. "I wouldn't say *that*... I just... I don't know."

"It's nice to believe in something," Tristan told me softly. "You feel safe. You have someone to talk to. There's hope."

"Why are you bad if you believe in God?"

He chuckled. "Just because you believe in God doesn't mean you're hardcore Christian. My parents are, but I'm not. I make my own path, I guess. I wish I were more religious. I regret not going to church as much, praying as much. Because I want to trust that I'm going to Heaven." He sucked in his breath. "And as said before, I don't like that I'm bad. It's just who I am. But if I believed in God more ... I don't know. Maybe I wouldn't be so bad."

I turned back to him. "Oh."

"Yeah."

"Well, you can choose whether or not you're a bad guy. Nobody is born bad."

He just stared at me. Blinked. He opened his mouth to speak but then a piercing screech interrupted our breaths and I found myself trembling. "I hate this," I whispered, my voice shaky.

"As long as we have the light, we'll be okay."

"I hope you're right," I mumbled.

"Don't worry. You'll be safe with me," he chuckled, grinning. "Goodnight, Skylar."

"Goodnight," I replied, gently closing my eyes. And not long later, Tristan drifted off to sleep. But I couldn't sleep. For hours, it seemed, I lay awake watching him. I'm sure that seems creepy, because it felt creepy, too. But I watched him and wondered what he was dreaming of. I imagined him robbing stores and getting drunk, but at the same time praying to God. There are secrets to everybody, apparently. Mysterious beyond everything.

The fire hummed throughout the cave and the screeches seemed to grow subtle, as if the creatures had drifted off to sleep, too.

. . . .

"Please forgive me."

I gasped, my eyes opening wide, my entire body in shock as a sharp piece of rock sliced through my thigh, a gash opening up and a heavy flow of blood seeping out. I watched the dark liquid pour from the open wound as I screamed out into the air. I couldn't breathe.

"I'm sorry. So sorry."

I glanced up to Tristan. His eyes were large and wet as he stared at me with so much guilt and shame I was sure he'd erupt in tears. But instead, he clutched the rock harder within his sweaty palm, stood up, and calmly left the cave.

Then everything went dark. And all that I was sure of suddenly vanished from my mind.

twelve

"What would you do if a zombie apocalypse started? Like, right now at this very moment."

Andria raised an eyebrow to me, then took a quick sip of her Shirley Temple. "What kind of question is that?" she asked, wiping the dribbles from her drink away with the back of her hand.

I shrugged, grasping my glass of lemonade tighter. It was so cold it was burning my skin, but I didn't feel like setting it on the table between our lawn chairs.

We were at Andria's lake house sometime over the summer. It was our hideout we went to occasionally, even though her parents were there, as well as her several waiters, chefs, and maids. We just called it ours.

Andria is rich, which is funny since she doesn't seem the type. Even though we go to the mall basically every weekend, she still ends up buying cheap stuff, or at least cheap-looking, like big shirts and leggings and sneakers. She has a near-perfect frame with a lot more meat on her bones than me, but she's a good sort of curvy. Her body is pear-shaped, so she's slim with wide hips. I tell her she should wear tighter shirts to show off her curves, but she's convinced she's too fat for that, which is *ridiculous*.

Finally, after Andria thought long and hard about the question I had asked her, she said, "I would push you out of the way and run away to find a hot guy." She smiled and looked at me, waiting eagerly to see my reaction.

I smirked. "Why a hot guy?"

"Well, so we could fall in love and fight zombies! *Duh.*"

"So basically *Warm Bodies*," I replied, sipping my lemonade.

"No, not *Warm Bodies*. That's not even close."

"It is a little."

"But yeah, I would definitely find a hot guy."

"What if he got infected, though?"

Andria drank from her Shirley Temple, analyzing the question. "He wouldn't."

. . . .

That next morning, I awake to the door being thrown open. I jump up, leaning back on my elbows on the bed. There stands Onyx, smirking, her hair a big heap of black madness, and her blue eyes stinging toward mine. "Good morning, dream-girl," she says.

I just blink. Behind her is a doctor rolling in a bed, and beside him is a nurse holding a bag of I don't know what.

"We're roommates now! Ugh, it's so stupid." She sighs.

I roll my eyes, falling back onto the bed, and turning over to face opposite of where hers is being positioned. "I don't need a roommate," I mumble.

"It will help you two to express emotions," the doctor tells us after the bed is placed in the right spot beside mine. "You can talk to somebody when Mrs. Carter isn't available."

"Whatever," Onyx says as she plops onto the bed. "*I* still don't need a roommate." The doctor and nurse leave the room, or so I assume. I can't see them, but I can hear the door open, then close, and all that remains is silence.

"Did you sleep well, dream-girl?"

I roll over to look at her and she's smiling at me. A creepy kind of smile. "Stop calling me that," I say.

"Nah, I'm good."

I sit up in the bed, pressing my lips into a line, just looking at her. My stomach growls.

"Let's go get breakfast," Onyx tells me, climbing down from the bed.

"We go out to get breakfast now, too?" I wonder, watching her walk toward the door.

"You can stay here if you want," she says, glancing back to me. "Dream some more."

I slip from the bed. "I'm not wearing a bra."

"Me either, but who cares? I'm sure Caleb will like it, though." Then she laughs an actual, real laugh, and it's weird against her oddly deep-ish voice.

I follow her out the room and toward the cafeteria, an uneasy feeling pressing on my shoulders. *What a strange person.* I stare at the floor and avoid her sharp gaze on me.

At breakfast, Onyx once again grabs nothing but an apple. Not even a drink. I, on the other hand, pile my plate with eggs, bacon, and cantaloupe, so glad I don't have to eat the soggy cereal the nurses used to feed me in the mornings.

"Why only an apple?" I ask Onyx as I fetch some chocolate milk from a bucket of ice.

She looks toward me. "You have a problem with apples?"

I raise an eyebrow. "Huh?"

"Don't ask me that again." Her tone grows harsh.

"Ask you what?"

"Just shut up," she lashes out, then turns toward the same table as yesterday and makes her way to it. I follow her with an awkward, yet confused expression on my face. *Yep, definitely strange.*

I realize then that I'm no longer uncomfortable in the cafeteria. Sure, it's still crowded, but I'm definitely not as nervous.

We arrive at the lunch table, and Caleb looks up at me and smiles. "Hello, Skylar!" He doesn't even acknowledge Onyx.

"You're pretty loud and happy for someone with anxiety and depression," I say to him flatly as I slide into a chair and set down my tray.

"He likes you," Jordan informs me. "*Duh*."

Caleb's face reddens and he frowns, turning to Jordan. "I barely know her!"

Jordan shrugs, smirking before sipping her orange juice.

I notice Onyx at the far end of the table, looking at a nearby wall in a daze. She bites into her apple slowly and carefully. "What's the deal with her and apples?" I whisper, nodding toward her.

Everybody shrugs.

"She's never told us," Caleb tells me. "But it's the only thing she eats."

"She got mad at me when I asked her about it," I mumbled, scooping a spoonful of eggs into my mouth. I didn't notice until now how much I had missed eggs.

"Yeah, never ask her about anything," Carol murmurs, her thin voice barely even audible. "She—'

"She's odd," Jordan says, interrupting Carol with her fierce tone.

I glance at Onyx again but she's not paying attention to us, her mind obviously somewhere else.

I hear giggling then. I turn to see Jordan and David obviously playing footsies under the table. They are both smiling and blushing. "Didn't you say you had a boyfriend?" I ask Jordan.

She turns to me, her expression suddenly cold. "Boys don't like freaks," she explains, sighing.

"Not true," David says to her.

Jordan glances at him and smiles.

I think about Tristan then and wonder if he were to see me now, would he treat me differently? Now that I'm in the place of the freaks? I remember his eyes, his smile, the feeling of his touch....

"Skylar?"

"What?" I spat out, shaking my head. I find myself staring at Caleb.

Caleb grins. "I was just saying it looks like you're happier today."

I give him a half-smile. "What makes you say that?"

"You're talking more."

I shrug. "I guess."

"Don't worry," he says softly. "Every day gets easier."

"Definitely likes you," Jordan repeats, laughing.

"Shut up!" Caleb snaps. And I find myself laughing with Jordan. It feels so nice to laugh.

. . . .

Apparently we only have group sessions every three days, but the individual sessions are still every day.

Today, Mrs. Carter seems tired and her face is worn. She wears less makeup, but that's not it. Something about her just looks sad. Even her normal bright outfit is bland today, with nothing but a navy blue shirt and gray pants. "Hello, Skylar," she says, her voice unnaturally chirpy. "How has your day been?"

"Everybody said I looked happier this morning," I tell her as I sit down, crossing my legs.

"You do."

I smile. "That's good, then."

She nods, smiling. But her smile sort of hangs there. I want to ask her what's wrong, but for some reason I don't let my lips utter such words.

"Now, yesterday was sure interesting. In the place, that is," she tells me.

"Yeah," I say, slightly laughing.

"I'll admit I was thinking about it a lot last night. How do you feel about Tristan betraying you as he had?"

"Well," I begin, "I was devastated. But don't worry, it's not over yet."

"Has anyone ever betrayed you like that, besides Tristan?" Mrs. Carter wonders, tilting her head to one side.

I swallow, then nod, dark images entering my head and clouding my thoughts.

"Who?"

"Andria."

Mrs. Carter raises her eyebrows. "Haven't we talked about Andria before? You two had a fight over a guy?"

I nod again, pressing my lips into a line.

"Would you like to tell me what happened?"

I stare at her blankly. "I don't know," I say. "I don't... I..." I look down to the floor, my hair falling across my face.

"You don't have to tell me now," Mrs. Carter says gently.

My eyes flick to hers. "No. I need to get it off my chest."

. . . .

I remember the day so clearly. It had been two days before the night of the happening. Matt and I had been apart for a little over three months. And I felt sick.

I called Andria and told her I'd be missing school.

"Aw," she whimpered. "Get better. I'll stop by your apartment after school to bring you soup."

"Love you," I said.

"Love you too, Sky."

But then around eleven I began feeling better, so I decided to go to school. I have always been the type to love school, especially math. I'd rather go to school than lie around and watch TV. I didn't tell Andria I was going, however, for I wanted to surprise her.

I walked to school. I remember the cold air biting my skin because I foolishly wore running shorts even though I knew it was thirty degrees outside. But I had a jacket.

It was lunch so I headed to the cafeteria after I checked into school. Andria wasn't in there so I walked around the halls, looking in all of her classes trying to find her.

Then I heard giggles and soft voices coming from a nearby hall upstairs. I turned a corner, and then I saw them. My best friend and ex-boyfriend, cuddling in the hall on the floor, holding hands. I screamed. They turned to look at me, their eyes wide.

Andria stood up quickly, her face full of fear. "Skylar! I thought you were sick!" Her voice trembled.

I glanced between her and Matt, too shocked to say a thing, or even cry.

"It's not what you think. We were just... we just... we were—"

"We've been banging behind your back," Matt blurted out, smirking.

"Matt!" Andria screamed, turning to glare at him.

He shrugged. "It's true."

I took a few steps back, and that's when the tears began to fall.

"Skylar, please—"

"Stay away from me!" I screamed.

"But—"

"Stay away, you filthy whore."

Her eyes widened. "I'm not—"

"Can you leave us alone?" Matt asked me harshly. I looked at him. "Yes, we were dating while you and I were dating. And yes, we've been together this entire time. But you're just embarrassing yourself now. Sorry, I'm sure it sucks. Andria is sorry, too. But please, just go. You're just making it awkward."

I turned and walked away then, slowly, too stunned to do anything more. I was completely numb. The tears fell, but I couldn't feel them run down my cheeks. I didn't know what to do. Andria called after me, but I never turned back.

That moment hurt worse than any slice to the thigh would.

. . . .

Mrs. Carter looks at me sadly. "I'm terribly sorry," she says softly.

I shake my head, forcing a smile. "It's okay. Definitely not one of my favorite experiences. But there's no way I can change what happened, you know?"

"Have you spoken to Andria since?"

"No," I say, clenching my jaw.

"Everything happens for a reason," she tells me, offering a closed smile. "I'm sure there was a purpose for this."

"Like what?"

"Like now you know how bad of a friend Andria was," she says. "And now you can move on from her *and* Matt, and branch out. Meet others. It's a huge step in your life. You just can't see it yet."

I smile at that. "Thank you. I hope you're right."

thirteen

I lie on the bed that night, staring up at the ceiling. I didn't think I'd ever be able to talk about what Andria and Matt did to me. Mrs. Carter is the first person I told -- besides Tristan, of course. But recently I've wondered if Tristan even counts.

I want to cry, remembering what had happened that day, with Andria and Matt, but because Onyx is directly beside me, I hold it in. So I just lie there, reliving the moment over and over again until it doesn't feel real anymore.

Onyx is watching reality TV. I haven't watched TV in forever. I always had the chance to while being here, but instead I spent the days by myself thinking deeply about the current situations in my life.

I sit up in bed, forcing myself to watch the television in order to get my mind off the pained memories of Andria and Matt. *Matt.* Even thinking his name makes my blood pressure rise even higher.

"Welcome back to the real world," Onyx says.

I'd look at her but my eyes are suddenly fixated on the TV.

"I'm sorry about what happened," I murmur.

"What?"

"When you were a kid." I turn back to her. She's looking at me now. "About your dad."

She shrugs. "Thanks, I guess."

I nod.

"You're nice," she says, her eyes lightening.

I grin. "Thanks?"

"You're tough and cold, yet you're nice. That's a good thing." She turns back to the TV. "Sadly, I'm just cold."

I want to say "and strange," but I don't. "Why do you watch reality TV?" I ask instead.

"You don't watch it?"

"Never."

She shrugs again. "I like it because it's fake, but at the same time it's more real than everything else. I love watching people live, and I love exploring their lives. I've always been envious of others' lives because mine sucks."

"Don't be envious of mine," I whisper. "Mine has nothing but abandonment and betrayal."

"But I promise you, every life is better than mine."

We watch a little bit more of the show in silence before Onyx says, "I'm tired."

"Me, too," I mumble.

She turns off the TV. "Good night, dream-girl."

I go to bed still thinking of Andria and Matt. I wonder how they're doing now, if they're happy. Probably. I doubt they care about me at all. And I eventually fall asleep with their faces still haunting my thoughts. I'm somehow comforted knowing there's somebody beside me while I sleep. Somebody possibly going through the same ache as I am, and probably being haunted by assumptions as well.

. . . .

I dream of myself. It is the same day in my dream, yet under diverse circumstances. I can immediately tell that I had never gone to the forsaken world. I am happy, I think. I'm smiling, anyway.

I then see Andria. She looks as beautiful as ever and beside her, I look even paler than I already am, my frizzy red hair an animal compared to her straight, black locks. We're laughing, but I don't know what at. I don't know where we are, either. We're in some sort of building. It's warm, the toasty air wrapping around me like a blanket. But an extreme uncertainty continues to creep over me.

That's when I spot Tristan, standing across from me on the other side of the building, talking on the phone. His hair is slicked back and he wears a uniform for boarding school, I think. A formal outfit with navy blue slacks, a cream dress shirt with a school logo on the upper right side, a navy blue tie, and black dress shoes. He looks much older, in his middle twenties or so. He appears more mature, his eyes more shapely, his thin lips slowly speaking into the phone. He runs one hand through his hair. He looks my way, but I don't think he sees me because he turns back to gaze toward a wall. But despite his odd maturity now, it's definitely him.

"Tristan!" I scream his name, running toward him. He looks at me again, his eyebrows furrowed as he watches me near him. Andria calls after me but I keep running. When I reach Tristan, I grab his shoulder, smiling ear to ear.

"What the hell?" he shouts, stepping back and lowering the phone. "Get off me!"

I give him a confused stare, my cheeks heating up. "Tristan? It's me, Skylar. Don't you remember me? From the world?"

"Are you crazy or something?" he snaps. "No, I don't freakin' remember you. Would you get away from me, *please?*" He rolls his eyes and raises the phone back to his ear. "Hey, Sam? Yeah. Sorry about that. This weird chick just attacked me." He sends me one last glare, then strolls away, leaving the building, and never looking back.

I stand there, my eyes puffy and filling with tears. Andria appears at my side. "What just happened, Sky? Who is that? He's cute."

"He's nobody," I mumble, bowing my head. "Come on, let's go."

. . . .

I wake up suddenly, my breathing quick in short, individual puffs. I turn to look at Onyx's bed but she's not there. I carefully sit up, swinging my legs over the side of the bed and leaning forward, my palms pressed to my knees. I shake my head, telling myself it was only a dream. Because of course, everything is a dream nowadays.

"Nightmare, dream-girl?"

I turn around to see Onyx curled up in the corner of the room, her cheeks stained with fresh tears. I'm surprised I notice because of how dark it currently is in the room. I nod carefully. "You?" My breathing is still harsh.

She doesn't say anything.

I stand, cautiously walking over to her. I slide down the wall, sitting beside her on the floor, wrapping my arms around my knees.

"I wish I had dreams," she tells me.

I look at her. "You don't have dreams?"

She shakes her head, then pauses. "I mean, you could say they're dreams. Technically they are, but to me they're memories. They're not made up. They actually happened. You know what I mean?"

"Is that why you were so harsh to me on the first day?" I ask her softly.

A sad laugh. "I guess so, yeah."

"It wasn't a dream I experienced," I tell her.

"How do you know that?"

"I just know," I tell her.

"Great explanation."

"Shut up," I tell her. She laughs again, not as sad. "But seriously, you know when you have those dreams where everything seems real? It feels *so* real. It's as if it's a sign of some sort. Like your boyfriend walks up to you, your best friend at his side, and tells you, 'everything is a lie.' You can feel his breath on your face as he says it. And you feel so stupid when you find him and your best friend together one day, because you never took that sign literally."

I inhale a deep breath. "Or you see your father in Georgia with a beautiful woman and a baby in a huge house. It's his new baby's birthday. It's a boy. Everyone is happy, eating cake and exchanging gifts. But when your birthday comes around, you don't even get a call. You don't get a cake. You don't get anything from your own mother. The only thing you have is your so-called best friend, but she's busy that day. And strangely, so is your boyfriend. And you don't realize until months later that they were both together, having fun, while you were at home alone on your freakin' birthday."

I look to Onyx; she stares at me wide-eyed. "You may think that your life is awful. And to be honest, I'm sure it is." She smiles at that. "But my life's hard, too. Everyone's life is hard. Everyone has flaws. So just because I'm a dream-girl, and you got molested by your dad… it doesn't mean you have it worse. You just have it bad because of a completely different reason than I."

She's still smiling at me. "You're actually really cool, Skylar."

I grin. "Thanks." But then my face grows cold. "Stop crying, please."

She wipes away her tears with the back of her hand. "I don't cry."

I laugh. Then she laughs. I don't even know why we're laughing at this point.

"But," she says, slicing through our giggles, "your best friend was really banging your boyfriend?"

I nod, pressing my lips into a thin line. "They had it all planned out, too. He started treating me like crap. She convinced me to end it with him. They wanted to be together, just them." I swallowed. "So I broke up with him. And while I was crying over him, she would hold me. But a few hours later she'd go over to his house."

"Dang," she says. "I'm sorry." I nod, looking at the floor. "But hey, I can be your best friend now."

I turn to stare at her, eyes wide. "What?" But I'm quickly smiling.

"I don't have any friends. We can be friends."

"I thought you hated me. And besides, what about Mrs. Carter?"

She wrinkles her nose. "What did I tell you? Hating is for wimps. I just thought you were really annoying. And Mrs. Carter is our counselor. It'd be embarrassing if she were our best friend."

"True, I guess," I laugh.

"So, you want to be friends?"

I smile. "I thought we already were."

. . . .

"So," I say, with eggs still in my mouth, "biggest fear."

"Definitely being too fat," Carol replies softly. I look at her plate, which has triple the amount I have. Apparently the doctors make sure she eats more than enough to gain weight.

"Heights," Caleb says, biting off a piece of bacon.

"Uh, zombies," David murmurs.

"*Zombies?*" Jordan laughs.

"Oh, you going to laugh at me now?" David smirks. "What's yours?"

"Yeah, Jordan," Caleb says. "Spill."

"Getting mugged," she whispers.

We all laugh. "That's not even a fear," David says.

"Yes, it is!"

"Skylar." Caleb turns to me. "What's yours?"

I press my lips into a line. "Uh, well… I don't know."

"Girl, you have to answer," Jordan says. "You're the one who picked this one."

I smirk, pressing my hair behind my ears and setting my elbows on the table. "Perhaps… realizing that the world I visited was really nothing but a dream."

Everyone is quiet.

"Specific," Caleb says, finishing off his bacon and licking his fingers. I nod.

"Mine is death," Onyx chimes in, and we all turn to look at her. She's decided to sit with the group today, right beside me.

"I'm not scared of death," David says.

"Neither am I," Jordan blurts out quickly.

"Good for you guys," Onyx mumbles.

"I'm religious," David says, "so I believe in heaven."

"That doesn't make sense," Carol counters. "If you kill yourself you go to hell."

David shoots her a rude glare. "Well, when I tried to kill myself that wasn't really on my mind."

"Yeah," Jordan snaps at Carol. "Don't judge someone if you don't know what they went through."

"I wasn't judging," Carol whispers, bowing her head.

"Yeah, you sort of were," Jordan barks.

"*So*," Caleb blurts. All heads turn to look at him. "David. It's your turn."

"Favorite color," he says with a shrug.

"That's freakin' boring," Onyx states. "But mine is black."

"Blue," Caleb says.

"Red," David says.

"Yellow," Jordan says, somewhat proudly.

"Sunset orange," Carol murmurs.

All heads then turn my way, waiting. I picture myself cuddling beside Tristan on the couch that first night. "Eyes…," I mumble.

"What?" Onyx asks.

"Green," I say quickly, my eyes suddenly wide. "It's green."

"My turn." Jordan leans forward, an evil smirk suddenly on her face. "Last person you kissed." She turns to David.

My stomach sinks and I hold my breath. My hands tremble, so I clasp them together and set them in my lap.

David looks toward Jordan, grinning. They stare at each other wildly. "Ours is easy."

"Ew," Onyx says. Jordan and David sharply turn to her. "Mine was a smelly boy with greasy hair like a month and a half ago. His name was Micah."

"Ew," Jordan says, mimicking Onyx.

"*Hey*," Onyx snaps. "He was actually a really good kisser. He had huge lips."

"I've never kissed a boy," Carol whispers, her thin fingers finding themselves between her lips as she gnaws her nails raw.

"My ex-girlfriend," Caleb adds coldly, eyeing me and only me. "Her name was Lily and she was amazing. But she dumped me about half a year ago because she met somebody else."

All eyes on me. I'm last again. I open my mouth to speak, but all that comes out is a croak. Caleb raises his eyebrows slightly, leaning forward, utterly intrigued. Everyone waits patiently.

I close my mouth and swallow. "I'm sorry," I murmur. "I can't answer this." I look at everybody as they squint at me. I stand from the table. "I need to go to the bathroom."

Nobody calls after me. Nobody even questions it. I think it's because they understand.

Some things just cannot be answered.

. . . .

"I can't get him off my mind," I say.

Mrs. Carter eyes me carefully. "Why is that?"

"I don't know," I mumble.

She sends me a sincere smile. She doesn't appear as cold today, her smile not as droopy, and her eyes not as dull. "That's normal, though. It's normal to meet a guy and then miss them."

"But nobody understands what I went through! I met a guy, and everybody is telling me that he is not real!" I grit my teeth, shaking my head. My fingers tighten on the chair as I lean forward. "He's real. I *swear* he's real."

"I believe you," Mrs. Carter tells me, her voice soft and soothing. "I promise. I believe you."

I glance up at her.

"I believe you," she repeats, smiling. "Now, where did we leave off?"

fourteen

When you wake up alone in a cave with a gash in your thigh, you sort of have to ask yourself, "What the hell is the point?" And as you lie there beside a pile of blackened bark that once was a fire, a fire that sent you warmth just the night before but now is vanished, you begin to analyze the question until you have to convince yourself that there *is* a point, for the fire within you is still—at least dimly—lit. And you don't want to become a pile of blackened bark, absent of any light.

I tried to stand, but it was so hard. I continued to fall back down, everything around me blurry for my eyes were filled with tears. I had so much ache within that I could barely breathe. I was too confused, too pained to answer the million "why's" suffocating my mind.

I then remembered the shirts I had put in my backpack. I reached into the bag and pulled one out, as well as the alcohol, carefully cleaning the wound as I bit my lip so hard a stream of blood began pouring from the corner of my mouth. The wound was so deep the cold air nearly breathed against my bone. How had just a small rock done so much damage? I didn't even want to think about it. I didn't want to remember it. The thought made me sicker than the wound.

Once I tautly tied the shirt around the bloody gash, I tried to stand up again. I made it that time, but I had to lean against the wall. I began limping out of the cave, grabbing my bag on the way out. It took me several minutes to make it to the opening.

It probably would've been better if I just stayed in the cave until the gash healed, copying Tristan's actions to make fires. But I knew I wouldn't last long. And I wanted revenge. I wanted to find Tristan again and cut each of his thighs.

The air smacked me hard in the face as soon as I entirely made it outside, the wind biting at my nose and fingers. I carefully limped forward to the road, slinging my bag over one shoulder. Every step I took hurt worse than the one before, a burning sensation devouring my entire body for a split second, and then subsiding into a hundred bee stings. I was tempted to crawl, but I knew limping would be quicker.

I walked—as best I could—in silence for a while, which was hard because my thoughts kept flicking to Tristan squatting over me, guilt in his eyes as he grasped that rock. What was he *thinking*? What was his purpose? I had a feeling I'd never know.

Suddenly, I fell, crying out before rolling onto my back. I was giving up. The pain began to rise in my chest, and I felt myself getting sick. For with this ailing feeling -- as well as the extreme dizziness that made my surroundings appear as a watercolor painting -- I knew I wouldn't make it. I would die. I was surprised I hadn't bled out already, literally *and* mentally.

That's when I heard a noise. Strong *clomps* on the ground. The earth beneath me shook as I sat up quickly, peering around until I saw multiple figures on the horizon. They were black, shaped as horses, running right toward me.

I didn't get up and run; I think it was because I just had no more energy left. I watched the figures as they grew nearer and nearer. My pulse sped up, but I just sort of watched them in a very calmly manner, pressing my lips together. My thigh had a heartbeat.

Eventually, the stallions halted and began casually walking to my side. I gazed up at them, wide-eyed.

Hello, Skylar, the obvious leader said to me through my mind, just as the cats had. His voice was strong and manly. Tough, but not in a scary sort of way. *You are far from your friend.*

The horses were jet-black, with emerald eyes and white swirls across their sides. I watched as one to the right of the leader stomped and scraped his hoof against the ground, as if he were claiming his territory, as if I could somehow take it from him. Another shook his head. These creatures actually had hair, despite the cats being made out of nothing but slick gold. Their black manes blew with the wind as they stared me up and down. Had they never seen a person before? It seemed as though they had already encountered Tristan, so I knew he couldn't have been far.

Why is your friend absent? the leader asked me softly, bowing his head.

My eyes flicked to his. The moment I looked him in the eye, my body filled with a soft warmth. "He's not my friend." My voice trembled. I didn't realize until then that I was afraid. But why didn't I feel as so?

But Skylar, the stallion hummed, *betrayal isn't always the end. Certainly not to a friendship.*

I frowned, pointing to my thigh. "He did this to me!" The stallion just stared at me blankly. I sighed. "He was never my friend. I barely knew him."

There is a purpose behind everything. Perhaps you have not yet encountered his purpose. Then he sort of jerked his head to the left and nodded. I knew what he wanted me to do.

I stood once again, the pain even harder to bear this time. I gritted my teeth, my eyes growing puffy. The horse leader strolled to me to lessen the distance between us. Then I gripped his soft mane and somehow managed to swing on top of him with my good leg. I straddled his back, holding onto his mane for support. I had never ridden a horse before but for some odd reason, I felt comfortable upon his spine, as though I had ridden them all my life. I leaned forward when the leader, as well as the rest of the pack, began galloping in the same direction I was limping toward earlier.

"Where are you taking me?" I wondered so softly I was sure he hadn't heard, but I was mistaken.

To the end of the world, he said.

. . . .

I woke up. Had I fallen asleep? I supposed I had.

The horses had halted. I peered forward to see a large amount of wild trees that appeared to be some sort of rainforest. I blinked. Why had they stopped? They hadn't expected me to walk the rest of the way, right? But they didn't say a thing, and they were frozen stiff.

There are five realms, the horse I was mounted upon told me at last. *Currently we are in the Realm of the Green. Before us is the Realm of the Forest. Then there is the Realm of the Sea, the Realm of the Snow, and the Realm of the Sand. Within one of the last three realms lies a hidden door, which we call the End of the World, and you must find it.*

"Why?" I asked, looking to the forest with furrowed eyebrows.

Because it is the end. You must hurry. You do not have much time. Sadly I cannot continue with you, for the other realms do not belong to me.

"What is this place?" I cried. At that moment I wished I hadn't fallen asleep so I wouldn't be in such a rush to obtain answers. And the gamut of realms frightened me. Why did there have to be so many? Why couldn't I have just gone to the End of the World right then? The stallion could've broken the rules, right? I mean, this place wasn't Earth. Rules could be broken here; rules could be broken among an unknown world… a possibly unreal world.

The stallion never answered me; he simply stood stiff again, frozen.

"Do I have to leave now?" I asked him.

I'm afraid so. There is no time to waste.

I slid from the statue-like horse, wincing as I landed on my wounded leg. I peered up to the horse leader and his green eyes bored into mine, sending cold shivers down my spine. I swallowed as he bowed his head to me. "Thank you," I said to him softly.

Good luck, he replied, trotting backward. *And the door to the End of the World is not where you would expect it. If you're looking closely, stop. If you think you've found it, you haven't. Farewell, Skylar Vail.*

The majestic stallions then turned and galloped into the green valleys. I was left alone once again, standing beside a humid forest with my thoughts racing within my head until they subsided into a mellow hum. And I descended into the forest.

. . . .

I had never been in a forest before. Obviously there aren't many around New York City, and Mom never liked hiking or anything. And even if she did, she probably wouldn't take *me*.

The rainforest was so awfully humid. I wiped away the sweat on my forehead with the back of my hand, but then more would appear, so eventually I gave up. I took off my father's rain jacket and tied it around my waist, my bare skin sticking to my T-shirt and leggings. I felt absolutely disgusting. I hoped the rainforest wasn't as huge as the endless green that I had just ventured through.

But besides the near-unbearable heat --which was very odd, because I was still used to New York winter-- the forest surely was beautiful. The trees were even greener than the valleys I came from, and flowers bloomed all around, which of course was bizarre, because as already stated, the icy air was present only minutes before. It was hot in the forest, the only hint of cold a subtle breeze. Luckily, I had shade from the sun because of the tall trees, but that only trapped in the humidity all the more.

And even when I was suddenly within a rainforest, brought there by wild stone horses who spoke to me telepathically about a door, I couldn't quit thinking of Tristan, which was annoying as heck. I was mad at him. I hated him. And that reminded me. Yes, my leg still ached... a lot. It wasn't as terrible to walk on it, and I wasn't limping as much, yet it still made me grit my teeth and squint. Although, after a while of walking, the pain seemed to blend into my uncontrollable thoughts of Tristan. Sadly, the memories of his green eyes, his cool voice, and the way he stared at me across the fire seemed to possess my mind.

I was gasping for breath among the thick, muggy atmosphere. I honestly didn't think I'd survive much longer there. Who knew what lay beyond the trees? Though it was silent besides my heavy breaths and the crunching of dead leaves beneath my feet, I felt an

unnerving sensation build within, as if someone were
watching me from above.

And also, peeing in a rainforest is not exactly an
easy thing to do. I was trying to hide, despite the fact that
no creatures were evidently present anywhere near me. So
going to the bathroom took up about thirty minutes of
my time. It was *awful*.

My calves were weak by the time the sun began to
set. Everything was sore, but I knew I had to continue;
the creatures would be out soon and there was still no
sign of shelter. I knew how to climb a tree, but did they,
too?

Somehow I'd forgotten I was starving with all that
was happening, so I fetched some of the old oranges
from my bag and one of the remaining bags of fruit
snacks.

As the sky darkened, I found myself beginning to
panic. And that's when I heard the screeches. I halted in
my steps, my heartbeat screaming from within. I was
completely out in the open, so in other words, I was
screwed. I bit my tongue and began looking around,
cursing under my breath, when I remembered the fire. I
quickly struggled to find some rocks and then began
furiously rubbing them together, yet no spark appeared.
Nothing happened except for the eruption of an *extremely*
aggravating sound. I cringed, sweating bullets, as though I
wasn't before. I started gnawing on my nails, too.

I heard a croak. I glanced up and there it was. A creature. But it wasn't as frightening as I thought it'd would be. In fact, it appeared human.

I stood up, so terrified I couldn't move, despite its unusually normal appearance. I felt entirely exposed, standing there before the creature. Of course, I *was* exposed, but I felt completely naked, my breathing so harsh my throat quickly grew raw.

The creature was a female. Young, probably close to my age, perhaps just a year older. Her skin was pure white like fresh milk, and her eyes, dark and pained, stared at me with so much intensity, as though I were a rabbit and she a large cat, her hunger consuming her. She started walking toward me then, not running, which confused me because they had chased after me twice before. The creature had brown hair—the same shade as Tristan's, actually. Her face was thin, but not as thin as you'd think an undead's face would be. If these things were zombies, they certainly didn't look it. Besides the darkened eyes and the white skin, they seemed pretty normal. However, the way the creature tilted her head to one side and was limping toward me, trembling, revealed she was not like me. She used to be a person, but then she was not.

Her expression seemed to soften as she neared me. She sniffed the air like a wild animal, looking me up and down. She seemed confused. I wonder what she was thinking at that moment. Was she trapped within that body? Or was she now an entirely diverse being?

Before I knew it, she stood directly in front of me. The lingering scent of death wafted from her skin and I winced. Why was she not attacking me? She grew closer, bowing her head toward mine. She was smelling me. I stood stiff, my arms at my sides. A tear trickled down my cheek.

She then made a purring sound, a dim vibration spilling from her throat. She stepped back, stared into my eyes one last, and then she sprinted away.

I swallowed, awfully confused. Perhaps she wasn't a full creature yet.

But even if that one didn't attack me, I was still not safe on the ground. I didn't care if the creatures could climb trees or not; I was going to climb one myself. And of course, I did. It was difficult with my wounded leg but I managed to climb it with at least a little ease.

I used to climb trees all the time with Andria. There was a giant one in the backyard of her lake house, and we'd climb to the very top at sunrise and sunset, either with a cup of coffee or cocoa, watching the sun do its thing. We wouldn't talk, just sit there in silence with the comfort of one another. And despite what Andria did to me, while I was climbing that tree in a rainforest, this memory comforted me.

I wasn't able to climb to the top, of course, but I made it pretty far up. I stopped as soon as I ran out of energy and positioned myself comfortably on a branch. I was high up enough to see the night sky so I stared up at the twinkling stars, biting my lip in order to somewhat lessen the pain of my leg. I wanted to cry, to curse to the night sky, but I stopped myself. There was no point in crying.

I remembered Andria holding me, Tristan holding me. They told me to let it out, that it was okay to cry. But both of them abandoned me. Both of them betrayed me. And that thought stopped me from crying.

My stomach growled. I supposed the oranges and fruit snacks didn't make too much of a difference. Thinking there had to be fruit up there in the trees, I began searching for some. And that was when I found a big, pink sphere on a vine above me. It glowed in the night. I picked it from the vine and ripped it in half, and juice spilled over my clothes. I was hesitant before taking a bite, but then again I figured I probably wouldn't survive in that world. For all I knew, I'd probably end up as one of the creatures, like the girl. So I took a bite and the soft, sweet fruit sent comfort throughout my body, settling my roaring stomach. It tasted like a mixture of an orange and a mango and a strawberry. I wished they had fruit like that back home, on Earth, where at that moment I was supposed to be.

I gazed into the darkened forest, wondering where Tristan was, wondering why the creature hadn't attacked me, and thinking of how delicious the fruit was until my thoughts eventually put me into a surprisingly sweet slumber.

fifteen

I stare at myself in the bathroom mirror that next morning before breakfast. At my thigh, right where Tristan cut me. There isn't a subtle scar visible, not even a line. I grit my teeth in aggravation. I don't understand why nothing has remained. Why isn't anything there? I close my eyes, sighing. *But it wasn't a dream.*

. . . .

"So today," Mrs. Carter begins warmly with a lipstick-coated grin smeared on her face, "we will talk about our relationships with others, what they really mean, and what they can do to us." Onyx groans, but Mrs. Carter ignores her. "So," she continues, "we are going to go around and each talk about our best friends." She nods toward Carol. "Carol, how about you start."

We all turn to look at Carol, watching as she bows her head, her eyes focused on the floor. "I... um.... My best friend's name is Shelby. She's very kind and pretty... perfect, actually. All the guys like her. *All* of them. And um, yeah, she was very close to me." She slowly raises her eyes to gaze toward Mrs. Carter, who seems somewhat pleased with this response.

"Now, Carol," Mrs. Carter begins slowly, crossing her legs and carefully leaning forward. "I know we've talked about Shelby before, but I would like the others to understand your situation." She then turns to stare the rest of us down. "Carol had anorexia, which means she used to starve herself to be skinny. Now notice how when Carol spoke about Shelby, she used the word pretty, and even *perfect*." Mrs. Carter then flicks her eyes back to meet Carol's cold ones. "But Carol, Shelby wasn't naturally perfect, correct? What did she do to have that perfect body?"

"She ate nothing," Carol mumbles. "She'd go days without eating any more than a single carrot. But she was happy doing it."

"She was?" Mrs. Carter asks.

Carol shrugs.

Mrs. Carter turns to us. "So you see, Carol's relationship with Shelby didn't completely cause her anorexia, but it still affected her. Do any of you guys believe that it's worth it to be a friend with someone who affects you negatively?"

Everyone shakes their heads.

"And also," Mrs. Carter continues, "we should *never* compare ourselves to others. Because there's no use! Someone may be skinner, smarter, funnier, but nobody compares to yourself." She smiles at all of us. "You are you, nobody else."

Mrs. Carter then turns to Carol once again, thanks her, and then looks to Onyx. Onyx understands that it is her time to speak before Mrs. Carter utters a word, and she quickly says, "Skylar is my best friend." A few giggles follow.

Mrs. Carter grins. "*Before* you came here, sweetie."

Onyx shrugs. "Then I didn't really have any friends. I sort of followed around wallflowers like myself. You know, I never really fitted in anywhere unparticular. I just sat around with a journal, writing poems."

Mrs. Carter nods. "Yes, writing is also considered a relationship, but with yourself. Would you like to share what you wrote about?"

Onyx swallows, suddenly uncomfortable. "I wrote about my pain."

"And did writing poems help release this pain at all?"

"A little. But it mostly just reminded me that I was pained."

"You should share a poem with us one day," Mrs. Carter says.

Onyx's lips curl into an uncomfortable smirk as though she ate something extremely sour.

"Well, anyway, thank you for sharing, Onyx. I'm sure we can all see how writing about pain and following outsiders can cause us to be more prone to depression by seeing others wander alone, and reminding ourselves that, as Onyx said, we are in pain. Am I correct?"

We all nod. Even Onyx.

"Caleb? You go next."

As I look at Caleb, I notice that he is heavily sweating, a palm pressed to his elbow. "I can't... today," he wheezes out. "Please, not today."

Mrs. Carter furrows her eyebrows to him. "What is the matter?"

"My elbow," he mutters, wincing. "And my throat... is... sore... and everything... *hurts*."

"Oh my, I'm sorry," Mrs. Carter says flatly. "But can't you at least share something with us?"

He swallows, gazing up at the ceiling. "I was... captain... of the... swim team. They were... my best buddies... all... of them." Caleb cannot stop swallowing, wincing, gripping his elbow harder. "But once... I got last place in my... 200-meter ... fly. And ever since... they quit treating me like... captain... because I... I... I...." His eyes find Mrs. Carter's. "I made them lose district."

Mrs. Carter nods. "Thank you, Caleb." She turns toward us. "So, Caleb's disorder is unique. It is usually formed because of a need for attention. Can you all see how Caleb, after being ignored by his swim team, began to search for attention? And as soon as he developed this disease, he got stuck within it."

Caleb nods quickly, gulping air like water and tapping his foot.

"Mrs. Carter?" Jordan asks bluntly. Mrs. Carter turns to her. "Why do we befriend people who hurt us? Like, why do we allow people to change us and make us depressed?"

Mrs. Carter opens her lips to speak, but I add in quickly, "We accept the love we think we deserve."

Everyone turns to me. "What?" Jordan asks.

I glance around to meet everyone's stares. "Has no one heard of that quote? It's from one of my favorite books, *The Perks of Being a Wallflower.*"

"I like that book," Carol murmurs, but everyone else just looks confused.

"That is very true," Mrs. Carter says quickly. "We do accept the love we think we deserve. And of course, this puts us in an even worse state most of the time, for with it lowers our self-esteem and causes us to believe that we *do* deserve this, which is not true at all." Mrs. Carter then looks me straight in the eye. "Skylar, would you like to talk now?"

I shrug. "My friends betrayed me… went behind my back and hurt me. There's not much to say besides that." I sigh. "It was all a lie."

Mrs. Carter nods. "And because of this, I'm sure your mind sort of collapsed, correct? This caused you to venture to another universe full of abandonment, where all of your worst fears came alive. Sometimes our minds will do that to us. They just break down because the wall of emotions is way too strong." Mrs. Carter glances around to everyone. "Friends alter our state of mind. What our friends do, how our relationships grow together, and fall, define most of our actions. So, because Skylar was betrayed by her friends, in her dream she was betrayed *several* times, her sadness consuming her, nearly possessing her. We have to be careful who we befriend, and we also have to be cautious as to how much we follow others for hope of having a friend. Do you guys understand?"

Everyone nods except for me, but I don't think anyone notices.

"Now," Mrs. Carter says softly, turning to David. "Would you like to go next, David?" And as he begins talking, I watch Mrs. Carter carefully. Her eyes look sad. Not as cold as they once had, but still sad. She seems young and vulnerable as she presses a strand of hair behind her ears, lifting her wrist. And when she does, the sleeve of her cardigan slides down, and there on her arm is a nasty black and blue and yellow bruise as large as a hand. When she notices, she quickly sets her hand back into her lap and swallows, and I begin to wonder if this lesson for us or for her. I swallow, my mind so suddenly sick that for the rest of the session I stare at her wrist and zone everything else out.

. . . .

"So, nobody else saw it?"

Everybody shakes their heads, yet their eyes remain distant.

"But it was *so* big," I wail.

"Why do you care so much?" David asks, sipping Dr. Pepper from the can.

I send him an evil glare. "Because she's a person, *too?*" I snap at him.

David shrugs.

"Does nobody honestly care but me?"

"Don't stress... about it... Skylar," Caleb wheezes. He still appears pained, just not as much.

"Yeah," Onyx says, biting from her apple. "She probably fell."

I stab my fork into my pasta. "Yeah," I mutter. "Probably."

. . . .

So that day in my individual counseling session, I ask Mrs. Carter about it. And when I bring it up, she almost looks mad. "*What?*" she asks.

"I saw a bruise," I say. "Are you okay?"

Her eyes grow puffy.

"Mrs. Carter?"

"I said to call me Susan!" she snaps. My eyes widen and she falls back into her chair, two fingers massaging her forehead.

"I ...," I whisper. "I'm sorry, Susan."

Mrs. Carter glances at me and smiles sincerely. "Let's just talk about you, okay?"

"But, Susan—"

"*Skylar,*" Mrs. Carter hisses sharply, her face then suddenly cold, her teeth gritted. "*Please.*"

I swallow and glance at the ground.

"Thank you," she says.

sixteen

I woke up that next morning with a stiff back and a crooked neck. I winced as the heartbeat in my wound began again, once my body gained consciousness. It was so silent—odd, of course, considering I was in a rainforest. Weren't there normally lots of animals in rainforests? It was even quieter than the day before. A whisper could be clearly heard from a mile away.

I carefully sat up, popping my neck. My hair was falling out of its bun, so I quickly redid it. I don't think my hair was even considered hair by then; it was such a tangled mess. Who would've thought I should've brought a hairbrush? I mean, I wasn't trying to impress anybody or anything, but I still wanted to be comfortable. But I knew that wouldn't happen because I felt so gross, wearing the same clothes for multiple days in a row. And I had a feeling there weren't any clothing outlets anywhere nearby.

I stood up, found some more pink fruit, and ate it, the sound of my bites slicing through the awkward silence. There wasn't even a breeze; it was utterly quiet.

Eventually, I made my way down the tree. Thankfully my wound didn't hurt as bad. I should've cleaned it, but as the horse told me, I was running out of time. Once I made it to the ground, I began to walk quickly through the rainforest, over the branches and the leaves, across the moist ground. It was hotter than the day before, my grimy clothes once again sticking to my wet skin. I panted as I walked. I was bored because it was so quiet, and I couldn't listen to music. I tried to hum, but it just wore out my dry vocal cords.

I began to think of the creatures. I wondered why the one from the night before didn't attack me, why it didn't climb up the tree to catch me. Perhaps it had to do with Tristan cutting my thigh? I began thinking about him again. Why would he want to hurt me? Did he not want me to catch up to him? I remembered his wound, how he winced and wheezed and tried to hold in his tears. Did that—

I froze. I saw him. Tristan. My breathing picked up its pace as I stared at him… his nearly limp, helpless body. He lay there on the floor of the rainforest, sweating bullets. He was breathing but his chest rose slowly. He was exposed. Just as I had hoped.

I fetched the nearest, sharpest rock I could find and cautiously made my way toward him, careful not to make a sound. I sucked in my breath, for surely I couldn't risk taking a gasp of air.

Am I really going to do this? I was but I was also unsure, as anyone would be. But he had hurt me, abandoned me. I couldn't trust him. It had to be done.

I was so close I could practically touch him. I could reach out, stroke his soft brown locks. I bit my bottom lip to hold in the tears. I doubted myself. Why was I doubting myself?

"Just go ahead and do it," he croaked, that familiar deep voice cutting through the air. I jumped up, screamed even. His scared green eyes stared at me and I swallowed. "Please," he said. "Just get it over with."

I stepped in front of him, grasping the rock tightly within my hands. He stared at me, helpless. He sat up against a tree as I lifted the rock into the air, my heart beating so quickly I was sure it'd explode.

"Give me one good reason why I shouldn't kill you," I snapped.

All the humanity suddenly vanished from his eyes like a single breath escaping into the wind. "There isn't one," he mumbled coldly.

I looked at him wide-eyed and scared, and he looked back at me, terrified. I could tell he was sorry. What was I doing? I began lowering the rock, but Tristan still sat there just as tense.

And that's when a gust of wind blew from the trees, and out escaped thousands of tiny black birds. They flew past me so furiously I dropped the rock and collapsed onto the forest floor beside Tristan, covering my head with my hands.

"We have to go!" Tristan shouted, grabbing my wrist and pulling me back up. He was suddenly awake, his expression wild, as though he wasn't just nearly lifeless on the forest floor. We had to crouch so the birds wouldn't knock us over. "Come on!"

I ran after him. My thigh hurt, but at that moment I didn't care about anything besides getting away from those horrid birds.

I covered my head with my hands again as Tristan and I sprinted through the forest, screaming as they picked at our skin. Blood trickled down from my shoulder, my calf, my sides, and my cheek. Their beaks stabbed both Tristan and me as though we were bird food, sharp pricks like a hundred jagged knives pricking our skin. Eventually the pain subsided because my fear overthrew it.

That's when we reached the ocean. I was surprised by how close it was to the forest; it was literally a line before us, the deep blue water only inches away. And Tristan and I both knew—we had to jump into the sea to get the birds off. The waves were violent in the distance, and I could smell the overpowering scent of salt. I don't think I had ever been so close to an ocean before then.

Tristan and I exchanged glances, then leaped into the deep blue water. I couldn't swim and struggled to keep myself up, and the icy cold water pressed me down and held me under, the waves keeping my body from remaining vertical. I panicked once my lungs realized I couldn't breathe. I couldn't see, either. I was petrified.

I felt Tristan then. He grabbed hold of my sinking shoulders and pulled me up with him, kicking fast. He evidently knew I wouldn't make it much longer without air.

Once we reached the surface, I gasped for air so violently I startled Tristan. He was treading water, and my arms were wrapped around his shoulders. He turned back to glance at me, then grinned. "Hey," he said.

I was breathing heavily. "Hi," I wheezed, smiling faintly.

But our hope almost immediately vanished when we heard a noise—a frightening howl from below us, under the water. We quickly looked down to see a figure among the blue, swimming toward us. Tristan began struggling to move out of the way, but he was too late. We screamed as the giant creature swam to the surface, carrying us high up into the air and then swallowing us whole.

seventeen

Onyx and I lay on our beds that night, watching reality TV. It has now become a normal thing to do this every night before we go to sleep. And I will actually admit that I sort of enjoy it, spying on others' lives. We watch anything from housewives to cooking shows to *Undercover Boss*.

But then I turn to Onyx. Her eyes are distant and her hair is oddly up in a ponytail. It looks better up than down, but I'm still not used to seeing it tied up and out of her face.

"There's something wrong with her," I mumble, and Onyx turns to me. "I know it. You know it, too. I can tell you've been thinking about it. You're thinking about it right now, aren't you?" She doesn't say a thing. "Why does nobody give a crap?"

Onyx sighs and looks down at her hands. "We're too sad," she says to me softly, almost as if she's embarrassed to admit it. "We're depressed, Sky. We can barely help ourselves." Her eyes flick to mine. "What makes you think we have the strength to help her? I mean, what would we do?"

"You guys aren't sad," I hiss, gritting my teeth. "You're just a bunch of selfish little cowards."

Onyx's eyes grow cold and she frowns. "You obviously don't understand what depression is," she says slowly.

"You're right, I don't. Because I don't have it."

"Then why the hell are you here!" she shouts.

I press my lips into a line, staring at her.

"You had a dream," Onyx snaps. "A *dream*. Everybody has dreams, Skylar." She breathes in and violently releases an exasperated sigh. "So who is the real coward here?" Then she turns back to the TV, a permanent scowl on her face.

"You have *no* idea what I've been through," I hiss at her. "No *freaking* idea."

Onyx spins back around to glower at me, her arms crossed in defense. "Maybe I don't," she whispers harshly. She breathes in deep and then furiously releases it, her eyes boring into me, yet somewhat distant. She's thinking about something else. But then her eyes readjust and she turns to the floor, her breaths shaky. "But what you went through wasn't real. What I went through *was* real. I went through it for most of my childhood, and it's still here." She turns to me again, her eyes glossed over. "My mom wants nothing to do with me, so I'm basically stuck here without a home. She trusted her own filthy husband over me, but when she realized *I* was the one telling the truth, she still chooses him." She shakes her head. "But you see? I'm still consumed by this madness. But you're done. It's over. You're not there anymore.

You're here. You're alive." She closes her eyes. "But the rest of us are dead."

I sigh. "Listen," I say. Onyx peers at me through squinted eyes. "I understand you went through a lot. I get that. And I already told you I'm sorry. But I'm still going to try to help Mrs. Carter. We have our own problems, but it's not like we're too busy to help the person who is helping us. It's like the golden rule: Treat others the way you want to be treated."

Onyx just stares at me, silent. The TV quietly hums within the darkened room, the light blanketing her with a vibrant glow.

"Is that why you named yourself Onyx?" I ask her. "It's a disguise, isn't it? You want to start over."

She nods, pressing her lips into a line.

"What was your real name?"

Onyx smiles bitterly. "Annabeth."

I smile. "That's a beautiful name."

She blushes. "But you can't tell anybody, okay?"

"You don't need to hide from your past."

"I'm trying to move on," she says bluntly.

"No, you're trying to forget. There's a difference."

Annabeth sighs. Perhaps calling her by her real name will help both of us from now on. You can't forget what happened to you, because you will always remain the same person. However, you can grow up, and you can be healthier and wiser. But your past is important, and I've learned that now. "Why are you trying to help me?" she asks, and I take my mind away from those deep thoughts.

"The same reason I'm trying to help Mrs. Carter," I say.

"You're an amazing person, Skylar." I grin. "Now let's watch TV." And so we do.

. . . .

Tristan is holding me. We're sitting in the middle of a field, a gentle wind caressing our skin. "I miss you," he says.

"I miss you, too," I reply. "When are you going to come find me?"

"Soon," he mumbles, somewhat distressed. "I'm sorry it's taking so long."

"It's okay," I whisper. "I won't let go of you. I just... I miss you."

Tristan buries his face in my hair. I can feel his warm breath on my ear and the tingling feeling sends shivers up my spine. I reach up and grab his wrist. "I can feel you," I breathe.

"Because I'm here," he tells me. "I've always been here."

"Then why haven't you found me?"

"You haven't found me."

And then he fades away until I'm left alone in the field, and the only thing remaining to hold me is the wind.

. . . .

"We're going to get it out of her," I say at breakfast.
"Whatever it is, we will get it out."

Caleb nods. "I saw it yesterday, too," he says. "I didn't question it, but she kept trying to hide it."

"Yeah," David mumbles. "I've seen it before, too."

"So, plan." Everyone's eyes dart my way, ready for me to speak. "Talk about relationships. Our relationships. Like dating-wise. We'll look at her eyes and wait. If she reacts, start asking her for advice. Don't overly talk about it, don't push it because then it'll be obvious. But if we all do this, it'll make her crack, and that way we can help her."

"But won't it be obvious if we *all* talk about relationships?" Annabeth asks.

"Onyx has a point," Caleb points out.

"Yeah," Jordan says. "She'll notice."

I nod in agreement. "Okay, two of us will talk about it. Tomorrow, two more. And two more after that."

"Why are you so desperate to help her?" Jordan asks, scooping a spoonful of eggs into her mouth.

"Golden rule," Annabeth answers for me, biting into her apple.

"We have to get her out of her relationship," I say.

"Okay," Caleb agrees. "I'll talk about relationships today. Who else?"

"I will," Jordan chimes in. "We normally talk about relationships anyway."

"Okay, good," I say. "Thanks, guys."

"No problem." Caleb smiles at me.

Annabeth elbows me when Caleb glances away. I give her a look.

Maybe this will really work.

. . . .

So that day during our counseling session, I notice Mrs. Carter's eyes are even more distant than before. And there is a mark on her neck that she tries to cover with a large, bright necklace. However, this only draws more attention to the blue of her skin. She scratches it stealthily as she smiles at me. "Hello, Sky," she says. "How are you?"

"Hi, I'm good," I respond, offering a thin smile and quickly glazing over her dull expression. "And you?"

She hesitates before answering, "Very good, thank you."

I remember Jordan saying she has her session right before mine, so I wonder if she said anything to Mrs. Carter, if she got anything out.

"Are we almost finished with the happening?" she asks me. "We've come a long way since we first talked about it, haven't we?"

I smile at this, actually. "Yeah, we're nearly finished."

"Afterward, you may even be well enough to go home."

I blink rapidly. "What?" For some reason, this frightens me. I hadn't really thought of ever going home.

I don't want to go home, back to Andria and Matt and Mom. I like it here.

"You okay, Sky?" Mrs. Carter asks me.

I nod, pressing a strand of hair behind my eyes and gritting my teeth. "I just… I don't want to go home yet," I tell her.

She nods, grinning. "You still have a little bit longer. But don't worry. When you do go home, the adjustment will be slow. And if you ever need to come back here for another day when things get hard, I'll be happy to have you visit for a bit until you're better again." She smiles. "And I'll find you a great counselor you can visit once or twice a week. How does that sound?"

"I want you to be my counselor," I mumble, my eyes wet.

"I'll still be just a call away. Always. But, of course, I'd love to continue to counsel you. I can always check in with the doctors. I'm sure you'd be much more comfortable with me still, huh?"

I nod.

She scratches her neck again and smiles weakly. "Ready to continue?"

eighteen

Just when I thought it couldn't get any worse, I ended up in a *whale*.

My eyes opened slowly and I peered around. It was dark, a slight glow coming from somewhere, and everything illuminated was red. I swallowed, cautiously sitting up. I was alone. I wondered if Tristan had also been accidentally eaten. *Accidentally*, I repeated to myself. I was so sure this whale was friendly and I didn't know why. Perhaps it was because I was still alive. If the whale meant harm, wouldn't I have already been devoured? But then again, technically I was.

I was covered in small, red bumps, perhaps from those horrid birds that literally flew from nowhere. I scratched the bumps; they were more like mosquito bites than bird pecks.

I pulled my knees to my chest. It reeked of fish and salt within the whale. This experience certainly wasn't ever on my bucket list, that was for sure. But it would be a fun story. I remember laughing to myself then. I was inside a *whale*. What a major turn of events.

But I wanted to look for Tristan. I wanted to find him, gently run my fingers through his hair, and listen to him tell me everything would be all right. So I stood and began strolling about the whale. It was wet but not humid, and I was very grateful for that. It was awfully disgusting, yet I somehow was not disgusted. It was as though I was used to all this weirdness by that point. Was I going to die? I don't think I even cared then. I just wanted to find Tristan.

"Hey."

I turned, my eyes wide. I saw him sitting there among the shadows, his face barely lit by that hidden glow. He looked tired—no, *exhausted*. He also had the same red bumps over his skin. He blinked at me as I stood facing him, twiddling my thumbs and swallowing a knot in my throat.

"Why didn't you kill me?"

"I was going to," I snapped.

A smile spread across his lips and I shivered, glancing away. "But you hesitated."

"So?" I flicked my eyes back to his.

"You were doubting yourself."

"I was," I admitted. "But that doesn't mean I was going to *not* kill you."

"Why didn't you?"

I gave him a look. "Well, I'm sorry. I don't know if you noticed, but a swarm of evil birds knocked me to the ground, and I was too busy trying to run away and save myself to kill you. I can kill you now if you want, though."

Tristan's smile faded and he stared at me with hardened eyes, sighing. "I'm sorry. You had every right to want to kill me."

"And why is that?" I asked. I had forgotten then why I had even wanted to find him. I should've stayed where I was. "Because you tried to kill *me*, too? Because if that's the case, no *duh* I did."

Tristan's face leaned forward into the light. He was growing impatient. "I didn't try to kill you."

"Well, you nearly did. So whatever you were trying to accomplish you did a really awful job at it," I growled.

"Why would I try to kill you and then save you from drowning the next day?" he asked sharply, his teeth gritted.

I just stared at him. "I don't know," I murmured.

"There was a reason behind it," he snapped, turning away. "I wouldn't do something like that to someone I had grown feelings for." My body shivered from those soft words he spoke. He turned back to me. "I'm a bad person. An evil person… and I'll admit that I've done some awful things in the past. But I wouldn't ever try to do anything awful to you." He shook his head, pressing his lips into a line. "Not to you."

"Then why the heck *would* you do it?" I cried out.

"Because I'm dying!" he screamed back, a red tint growing across his cheeks like a rash, his eyes narrowed and his body tensed with discomfort. "And I didn't want you to see me die! To turn into one of those creatures! Because I will turn into one. And I will attack you. I was trying to protect you, Skylar!"

I stared at him blankly, his reply frightening me. I slowly sat on the wet ground, crossing my legs and leaning forward. "*What?*" I whispered, my stiff shoulders dropping.

Tristan's scowl softened. "Those things are zombies. They scratch you, and then you turn into one. They scratched me. They gave me this gash. And I don't know how long it'll take, but every day is worse. Every day I become one even more. I can *feel* it." His eyes are watering. "Have you ever experienced the feeling of dying?"

It took me a moment to realize he was truly asking me. I thought back to when I saw Andria and Matt together, and my heart shattered all over again. But I inhaled a deep breath and shook my head.

"It's cold," he whimpered, his voice oddly cracked. "And it's quiet. And you can literally feel your body fading away."

"But you don't know you'll die for sure," I croaked. I was afraid, but why? I had wanted him to die just moments before. But did I really? I wasn't completely sure, and I was confused. I didn't want him to die. Was it because I had grown feelings for him? I guess I had. I bit my lip as I watched him study me.

"I *will* become one of those things, Skylar. I know I will."

"But why did you hurt me? So I wouldn't chase after you?" I snapped.

Tristan just stared at me. I knew it was a yes, and I swallowed.

"You didn't have to cut my thigh," I whispered. "I probably wouldn't have caught up either way if you had just left while I slept." But then I remembered the horses. I didn't mention them.

Tristan shook his head. "Once the creatures cut me, they ran away. They didn't kill me because they were done. So I figured if I cut you, you wouldn't be attacked because they don't harm the already wounded." He swallowed. "I didn't mean to cut so deep. When you woke up, it scared me and I accidentally sliced too much. I meant for it to be a subtle cut."

I remembered the one creature that approached me in the forest, purred, and ran away. She didn't attack me. Did that mean Tristan's theory had worked? My eyes trailed to the ceiling as I thought about it. Could Tristan really be innocent in this situation?

"Skylar?" My eyes flicked to meet his. "I'm sorry."

I breathed in deeply. "Why didn't you just *tell* me the cut was from the creatures? What would I have done?"

He shrugged. "I don't know. I was going to tell you. When I woke up after I had been attacked, I glanced over and saw you, and you were so beautiful, Sky. So beautiful." He smiled slightly, yet it quickly subsided. "But I *knew* I couldn't risk it. I knew what I'd become. And so I left, but you found me that same night. I almost left again, but then you found me outside. And I got to know you, and it became harder and harder to want to leave... I didn't want to leave, but I knew I had to. I didn't want you getting hurt because I had no idea when I'd change. For all I knew, it could have been any second. And all day I was so paranoid. And that night in the cave as I lay beside you, I felt something I had never felt before. I don't know what it was... I wanted to kiss you, be closer to you."

His eyes drifted downward and he blushed. "And I made a plan because I knew I couldn't stay. I didn't want to hurt you. And I'm sorry that I did. *Really* sorry." His eyes find mine again, wide with a deep meaning hidden among them. "But then you found me again." And he smiled.

I glanced away, licking my lips. Why was I giving into it? I shook my head slightly as I turned back to look at him. He was closer, carefully leaning in. My heartbeat picked up as his eyes found themselves at my lips and he licked his own. I swallowed and tilted my head forward as well. But then I stopped, sitting up straight. "I can't," I said.

Tristan peered up at me. He didn't seem sad or even embarrassed. He seemed to understand, actually.

"You're not even real," I said to him, biting my lip. "This place is so crazy it has to be a dream. I mean, am I right? It's a dream, isn't it? We're dreaming."

And I remember so clearly then that Tristan shook his head.

"Why do you think this is real?" I asked softly.

He grabbed my hand, caressing it softly with his thumb. A vibrant warmth shot through my veins, and it felt so wrong, yet so right. My lips parted slightly as I waited for an explanation.

"Because," Tristan told me, "you feel so real." He smiled. "And besides, I think I've figured it all out."

"You have?"

He nodded, sitting up straight. "You see, this place holds everything we're afraid of. I believe in dimensions… and we each came here during our sleep, right?" I nodded. "I think we got trapped. I think while we slept, we dreamt of our fears, and ended up here."

I gave him an odd look. "So it *is* a dream?"

"No," he said. "It's an alternate reality in our heads."

"So basically a dream."

"No, there's a difference."

I bit my bottom lip. "If this is a place of our fears, then how'd we end up in the same reality?"

"Because our minds are alike," he said. "We've each been betrayed. We're wallflowers… we've never fit in. We are abandoned and we're—"

"We are forsaken, Tristan."

A thin smile spread across Tristan's lips like butter over warm toast, melted and creamy. "Exactly," he said.

"So we're trapped," I mumbled. "We're trapped in our heads… how?"

"Our minds, Skylar, are so vast. We're thinkers. We stand back and observe. We're unlike others and because of that, we understand things in a different way… so we ended up here."

I thought back to when the horses told me about the hidden door. I was about to tell Tristan about it when he said, nearly reading my mind, "Did you speak with the stallions?" I nodded. "Figured. They told me they had to leave to go back for you. I think the door is a test. They don't want other creatures entering other dimensions, so we have to take a test to see if we really do belong on Earth. And if we fail, we're stuck here."

"Gosh," I said, laughing. "How did you come up with all these theories?"

He smirked. "I was alone for a while in the forest." I stared at him. "But either way, it's only an assumption. A guess, really. I don't think we'll ever know for sure. Not me, at least."

I swallowed. "So what now?"

"What do you mean?"

I grinned. "We're in a whale."

He laughed. "Right. I guess we'll just have to find out eventually."

I smiled, nodding and then staring deep into the darkness of the whale. I wondered what part we were currently in. Was it the stomach? I didn't really want to know.

"Do you forgive me?" His cool voice startled me as I jerked my attention back to him.

I shook my head and grinned. "Though you can't blame me, really." His face grew cold. "But I don't want to kill you anymore, if that's something."

His smile reappeared, but it was thin and only remained present for a slight second. "Technically," he said bitterly, "I'm already dead."

"You better not die on me," I snapped, biting dead skin from the corners of my nails, loose hair from my awful bun falling over my face.

"I'll try not to. But I don't think I have a choice, honestly."

"Do you really think I'm beautiful?"

Tristan's eyes widened then, and he seemed embarrassed. He glanced away.

"Well," I said. "Thank you. No guy has ever called me beautiful in person before." His eyes found mine quickly. "And meant it," I added.

He smiled. "Well, you're beautiful, Skylar. And I mean it."

nineteen

"You have to break up with him, Sky. He's only making things worse."

"No, he's not," I barked at Andria as I twirled my spoon in my soup. "It's just... he's in a bad mood."

"Then he's been in a bad mood for weeks!" Andria yelled at me, oddly infuriated with me. "Let him go, Skylar!"

"I don't want to!" I screamed back. Then I paused and took a deep breath. "I love him."

She stared at me with a pained look. It was as though I was watching her heart break into a million pieces right before my eyes. And now I can't help but wonder how I didn't realize before. How I was so oblivious.

"Let him go," she whispered.

I began to sob, and she watched me, her eyes small but her mind in a different world. She was silent, pressing her lips into a line. I wonder now: what was going through her head as she watched me fall apart.

. . . .

It's my turn to talk to Mrs. Carter today. Mine and David's. His session is before mine.

"How did she react yesterday?" I ask Caleb at breakfast.

"She seemed sad," he replies. "I felt bad."

"That rhymes," Annabeth says.

"Maybe she'll crack today," I murmur.

"What do you expect to happen, Skylar?" Jordan snaps. "That she'll just *leave*? Who knows how long she's been married to him."

I shrug, eyeing her cautiously. "We'll see what happens."

. . . .

"Hello, Skylar," Mrs. Carter says, tucking a strand of hair behind her left ear and sipping her coffee gently. She appears happy today. *Happier*, that is.

"Hello, Susan. How are you?"

Mrs. Carter seems surprised by this question. Had I never asked her that before? I could've sworn I had the time before. "Good," she replies slowly as she sets her cup on the table between us. "It's been a good day. How about you? How are you?"

I suck my breath in deep. "Not so good," I say.

Mrs. Carter's face falls. "Oh no. And why is that?"

"I've been thinking about my ex-boyfriend a lot."

She presses her lips into a line. "What are you thinking about?"

"Well," I begin, "I have a feeling he's doing just fine without me, you know? He and my best friend are probably living it up, and they don't even care. It's as though I meant nothing to him."

"Why did you break up with him again?"

"Andria made me."

Mrs. Carter shakes her head. "No, Skylar. We all make our own decisions. There is a reason behind every action. You see, everything is a choice, whether we want to stay or leave. So, why did *you* leave? And it was not because of Andria."

"How was it not because of her?"

"She may have persuaded you, but she did not make the choice for you."

I swallow. "I guess she helped me see how poorly he was treating me."

"So why do you miss a guy who treated you so poorly that you had to end it with him?"

"Because I thought I was in love, but I'm not." My eyes flick to the floor. "I was using him for comfort. I enjoyed the feeling of attachment. I liked when he bought me things and called me pretty." My eyes find hers again. They are sad and glazed over with intense thought. "I was using him."

"*You* were using *him*? That's an interesting way of seeing it."

I nod. "I was using him for comfort. He was using me so he had something to control and to push around. "

Mrs. Carter's lips part slightly as though she wants to add something, but she's afraid.

"I guess I broke up with him because I realized what I was to him—a toy."

Mrs. Carter glances away. "It seems as though you've found an answer to your problem."

"Perhaps. I simply need to realize I'm better off without him. He was weighing me down and making me feel like crap." Mrs. Carter stares at me, her gaze solemn, yet soft. "So why am I still holding on to him, Susan?"

"Because I love him," she whispers. "I'm in love with the thought of loving him."

I furrow my eyebrows. "What?"

Her eyes widen. "Nothing."

I bite my bottom lip slightly. "He's hurting you, Susan," I tell her, my words smooth and slow, as though if I blow out too much air the force of it will snap her in half.

Mrs. Carter's surprised expression melts into a scowl. "Now, Skylar—"

"Stop it!" I scream at her, my pent-up rage suddenly exploding. My strong words frighten me a bit, but I continue anyway. "Stop denying it! Stop pushing it aside!"

Mrs. Carter's scowl digs deeper into her brow. "Don't yell, Skylar. This is my life. This is my *personal* life."

"I won't let you go home to him."

"Why do you care about helping me, Skylar?"

"Because you helped me!" Her expression lightens. "You basically saved my life," I tell her, my tone quickly warm and fuzzy. "You've saved every kid's life.

Every kid here was saved because of you." She looks at me and I can see her heart shattering in her distant eyes. It reminds me of how I saw Andria as she watched me cry; I can see Mrs. Carter's soul breaking as she realizes what she's done. "So why can't you just let me help you?"

"I'm afraid," she whispers to herself.

"Afraid of him?"

She nods gently.

"Susan, you have to leave." She looks away. "That's why you appeared in my room so quickly that one night, correct? You were in your pjs." Her eyes find mine again. "You know where to get coffee at night. How would you have known? Counselors don't work here at night. You stay here a lot when you're scared to go home, don't you?" She just stares at me. "Because he hits you."

Tears well up in her eyes. "Skylar...."

"You're pushing it aside, Susan! He's hurting you! He's killing you!"

Then she begins to bawl, pressing her face into her hands, and howling like a dying wolf. I slip from the love seat and crawl to her carefully; once I reach her I place my hand on her shoulder. She glances up, just watching me, waiting for me to speak.

"You're a wonderful person," I tell her. "Stop killing yourself for that feeling of attachment. It's not worth it. I would know."

A smile emerges beneath her tears and she bends down to hug me. We hold each other for a while as her sobs create a waterfall down my shoulder. I close my eyes as I embrace this moment. I have never helped someone before... at least not someone so deep in a single hole.

"I need to get help," she says, so softly I can barely hear, her voice wet from the tears. "I may need to take a few days off." I hold her tighter and then she pulls away, looking me in the eyes. "Thank you, Skylar. Thank you *so* much."

. . . .

"So," Annabeth says that night, completely shocked by what I told her about my day with Mrs. Carter. "She just... *agreed*... with *you*?"

"I'm a good persuader," I reply, smiling ear to ear. I squeal and press my face into a pillow, so much delight within me. I saved someone! I don't remember feeling this happy in... forever, as it seems.

Annabeth laughs. "Good job, dream-girl."

"She may take a few days off, though," I say, taking the pillow from my face and staring at her with a plain expression.

"So, what?" she asks. "We get a replacement counselor?"

I shrug. But then my smile reappears and I squeal again. "I'm so *happy*!"

Annabeth just laughs again.

I pause suddenly. "Why do you eat apples?"

She turns to me. "Because my sister ate apples all the time. They were her favorite." Her voice is suddenly cold.

"But why do you eat them?"

"Car accident," she replies bluntly. "Two years ago."

I stare at her blankly. "Oh, I…."

"Don't worry about it," she says, looking back at the TV. "It was a while ago. She's in a better place now."

I watch her expression harden as the lights from the television create a radiance over her skin.

twenty

Annabeth and I are getting ready for breakfast when Dr. Richards knocks on our door. I am staring at my reflection in the mirror, trying to figure out whether or not my white shirt makes me appear younger, when I jump at the disruption of my thoughts. I turn back to see Annabeth quickly slip on some shorts and open the door. "Yes?" she says.

Dr. Richards enters, casually strolling past her. He stares at me as I step forward, leaning against the frame of the entryway to the bathroom.

"I have good news and bad news," he says coolly, glancing between Annabeth and me. "Which would you like to hear first?"

"The bad," Annabeth mumbles quickly.

Dr. Richards smiles thinly at her. "Well, Mrs. Carter is having some complications at home." My stomach sinks at this. "She is actually not going to be here today, nor will she be here tomorrow or Tuesday."

"So, what's the good?" Annabeth asks abruptly.

Dr. Richards turns to me then, his smile widening, yet warily. "You will have the next three days as free days."

"Free days?" I whisper, narrowing my eyes.

"Free days!" Annabeth repeats, only with more exclamation.

Dr. Richards nods. "You kids have been through a lot, and I trust you all. Mrs. Carter was actually the one to recommend this. You all can tour the hospital if you'd like. We also have a playground outside. Or you can stay in here and do what you'd like. If you want a tour, I can fetch a nurse."

"There's no substitute counselor?" Annabeth asks.

Dr. Richards shakes his head and rubs the back of his neck. "No, because she'll only be gone for three days." He lowers his hand, then pops his neck. "We thought this would be more fun."

"Thank you," I mumble.

He smiles at me. "How about you guys talk to the rest at breakfast and see what you'd like to do."

"Okay," I say.

"Will do," Annabeth replies.

When he leaves, she and I exchange exciting glances, and we run to each other and hug. "You really did it, dream-girl!" she squeals. This is the first I've ever heard Annabeth so happy.

. . . .

As I walk to the table with my tray, everybody cheers. I blush and look away, a huge smile plastered over my lips. I set the tray down as they all individually stand and hug me, Caleb holding onto me longer than the rest. When I sit down, they can't stop blurting out questions like, "Why didn't you tell us last night at dinner?" or "How did she crack?" But out of respect for Mrs. Carter, I don't answer. Instead, I say, "Guys, what's done is done. And she's okay now."

They nod and smile and continue their meals.

"So what the heck are we gonna do today?" Jordan asks.

"I thought a tour would be cool," says Caleb.

"Me, too," David agrees as he takes a bite of his bacon.

"Yeah," replies Annabeth. "I was thinking that, too."

"Sounds fun," Carol mumbles.

"Okay," says Jordan.

They all turn to me. "Skylar?" Caleb asks.

I smile. "Why not?"

So after breakfast we freshen ourselves up a bit, which isn't easy, considering our clothing is limited to mostly T-shirts and PJ shorts or pants. I tie my messy hair into a ponytail, strands of it falling over my face. I put on a light blue shirt, a color that matches my eyes, because I agreed that the white shirt did in fact make me look young. Annabeth braids her hair over her shoulder, and I sit on the bed watching her.

"I never learned how to braid," I say.

"Really?" she asks, oddly surprised, looking me up and down.

"I mean, my hair isn't exactly braid-worthy."

Annabeth ties her fishtail with a ponytail holder and walks over to me. "May I?"

"Sure." I position myself so she can easily reach my hair. "How'd you learn to braid?"

"Lots of free time," she replies softly as she pulls out my ponytail holder. "I was grounded a lot." She tries to run her fingers through my tangled hair, but she can't. "Girl," she says. "What the heck."

"It gets poofy when I brush it." I laugh.

She fetches a hairbrush and starts brushing, but then it gets stuck and we erupt in laughter. She suddenly yanks the brush out. "Ow!" I scream.

"I'm sorry!" she howls. She runs to the bathroom and pours some water onto the brush, then comes back and tries again. The brush hurts at first, but once the tangles are mostly gone, it's very relaxing. I close my eyes as she runs her thin fingers through my locks, and then at last begins to braid. She finishes in about ten minutes.

I awake from my daze and go to the mirror, gasping at my reflection. I've never seen my hair so smooth and clean, and the braid is a loose French. My hair is much longer brushed, so the braid almost reaches the middle of my back. I pick it up and slide it over my shoulder so it hangs across my chest, and I smile. I look stunning.

"Thank you," I mumble.

"Anytime," she replies.

When we meet up with the rest by the cafeteria, Jordan says, "You guys took *forever!*" But then she pauses when her eyes meet mine.

"There's something different about you," David mutters.

"I like your hair," Carol says with a thin smile.

I look to Caleb. He smiles. "You look great, Skylar," he breathes.

I blush again. "Anna—" I cough. "I mean, Onyx did it."

"Yeah, yeah," Annabeth says. "I did a good job. Skylar looks pretty. Let's go!"

The nurse takes us basically everywhere except for the major trauma areas. We see the babies, the pediatric center, and we even get to visit the X-ray machines and the physical therapy room. The entire tour takes only about an hour when at least we reach a giant green field with tons of flowers, a giant playground in the middle. Like children we run out to the empty park and begin sliding down slides and swinging on the swings and climbing the monkey bars. As we play and laugh and smile, we all appear happy. We are healthy and free, even if we obtain a mental illness. And for a single moment, as I swing beside Annabeth and Caleb and I close my eyes, I forget I'm at a hospital at all. I forget I had a dream and I forget about Andria and Matt and Tristan and Mom, and I just swing. I feel the wind on my face and hear the squeals from Annabeth. I feel alive.

We play on the playground for nearly an hour before lying on the grass and staring up at the clouds.

"I see a bunny," Carol says.

"I see a dragon!" David shouts.

"I see a sky whale swimming through a rainforest," I mumble.

"Welcome to the land of the freaks," Annabeth purrs.

. . . .

That night, we find ourselves on the top of the playground, staring up to the stars. We talk about randomness and life, as if we're long-lost best friends. I don't think I've ever felt quite this happy in a while. We laugh, telling stories of our past, when we were normal. When we weren't suffering from these diseases that keep our thoughts locked away in our bodies.

Eventually, everyone decides to go get food and head back to their rooms. We left to get lunch earlier, but of course that was lunch, and now it's dinner. I don't want food, however, for I ate way too much a couple hours before and am still full, so I tell the others I'll stay at the playground. But then Caleb offers to remain with me. I tell him it's okay, that he could go, but he insists. Of course, I don't tell him to go with the others, but I nearly do. I grit my teeth and force a smile. Don't get me wrong; Caleb is friendly enough, but I'd much rather be alone and dwell upon my thoughts. And now that I think of it,

I haven't been alone in a very long time. Like *alone*, meaning by myself, talking to myself, finding myself. Have I even glanced once at what I've become and how I've changed? Not to anyone else… but *me?*

I turn to Caleb, but he's already staring at me. He blushes and looks away. We stand at the top of the playground, our hands clasped around the railings, swinging ourselves and glancing down at the ground. "It's a pretty night," he says to me sweetly.

"Have I changed?" I ask. "Since I've been here."

He stops swinging and his face grows cold as he studies me. "I mean, you look about the same—"

"*No*, Caleb," I say with a laugh. "I mean, me. My personality."

"*Oh*," he replies, smiling weakly. But then his smile fades and he shakes his head. "No, not really."

I frown. "Really? I haven't?"

"You haven't changed," he says, his eyes darting to the ground below us. "But I think you've let loose."

"What does that mean?" I ask bitterly.

He looks at me again. "That means I think you've just realized who you really are. Instead of following a crowd and being who everybody wants you to be, you have subconsciously realized that you are you and that you can do anything you want to do." He breathes in deeply. "Because you are a very powerful person, Skylar."

I stare at him, eyes wide. "Wow." A thin smile forces its way onto my face. "That's deep."

He chuckles. "I tend to say deep things."

"Why are you here?"

He blinks to me. "I have pain dis—"

"No," I snap. "You're always so happy. You're the happiest one here. I've only seen you in pain once. And you don't seem depressed." He doesn't say anything so I repeat, "Why are you here?"

He swallows and stares up at the sky. A dim chirp sounds in the distance—a cricket, I figure. "The pain is always there. I just have a good way of hiding it."

I furrow my eyebrows at him, even though he's looking away. "Why do you hide it?"

"Well, I try to ignore it. If I ignore it, it will disappear." He stares at me then, his bright brown eyes dancing under the light of the moon. "But it's always there."

"You can't ignore problems," I tell him. "They may go away and hide somewhere in the back of your head for a while, but it's pointless because they'll always find their way back." He just stares at me, biting his lip. "What is it?" I ask.

He smiles. "I've never met a girl like you before."

"Is that a good thing?" I ask, turning away.

He grabs my face and I'll admit, I am taken by surprise. He tilts my face toward his, looking me straight in the eye. "It's a great thing." And then he leans in closely, our noses nearly touching and my breath heavy. But I quickly pull away, stare to the ground.

"I'm sorry," I say. "I can't."

I hear him swallow. "No, I'm sorry—"

I look back to him. "I'm waiting for someone." His eyes widen. "I know it sounds stupid, but I lost someone and I'm still waiting for them."

He nods, pursing his lips. "Sometimes it's better to let go than to hold on." I frown, and he continues, "A tight grasp can do more damage than a wandering path." He scratches the back of his head. "I'm going back inside. Good night, Skylar."

And then he leaves, and I watch him carefully fade away into the shadows. I realize then that I no longer wish to be alone.

twenty-one

I sat at the kitchen table, twiddling my spoon in my cereal. The last "normal" day of my life until now. I sighed, pressing my fist into my cheek, resting on my elbow. My hair fell over my eyes, but I didn't push the strands from them.

My mother walked into the kitchen, rushing as always to get to work. She poured herself some coffee, staring at me above the cup. When she set it down with a *clink* on the counter, she spat at me, "Would you stop moping around? It's been what, three days?"

I just looked back at her, blowing air quickly from my nose. The milk from the bowl of cereal rippled with the flow of the spoon and a gentle splash could be heard. It seemed to relax me. I closed my eyes.

"So what?" she continued. "He's with someone else now. He's moved on. You should move on, too."

I opened my eyes slowly to peer up at her. I frowned, my stare cold. "You have no idea what I'm going through," I murmured.

She smiled. "As a matter of fact, I do. It happened to me many times. This won't be the last for you, either." She picked up her coffee and sighed as she looked me up and down. "Get ready for school already." And then she left.

I stared at the front door for a while. My eyes watered when I finally stood and poured my cereal into the sink. It was a normal day.

· · · · · · · · · ·

The next two days passed by quickly. David and Jordan hung out around the hospital, and Carol and Caleb apparently did as well. Annabeth and I didn't feel like taking another tour, and instead cuddled up in our blankets and watched sappy love films, commenting on their flaws and moaning during the kiss scenes.

I wanted to badly tell Annabeth about Caleb almost kissing me, as well as the words he spoke to me. Why did I not? Perhaps it was because I was embarrassed that I was still holding on to Tristan, confused as to what I should do.

But of course, she eventually figures it out. "So how was your night with lover boy, dream-girl?"

My eyes quickly find hers as she peers at me through the darkness. "What?"

She smirks. "You know what I mean," she purrs, turning back to the television.

"Nothing happened," I say quickly, pulling the covers up to my nose, grasping them tight.

She laughs. "Like I'm buying *that*. Come on, dream-girl. Tell me."

"*Fine*," I snap with a grin, giving in. "He tried to kiss me."

"I *knew* he was into you!" she exclaims. "You're lucky. He's *so* hot. Well, how was it? Is he any good?"

I stare at her, pressing my lips into a line. "*Tried,*" I murmur. She doesn't get it. "I didn't kiss him."

Her face suddenly falls, her expression irritated. "You *swerved?*" I nod. "Who in their right mind swerves *Caleb?*"

"Me," I mumble.

She just smiles, shaking her head. "You're insane." And thankfully this is the last of it. I'm glad she doesn't question me further, as I already feel bad enough, especially being reminded of it. But I doubt Caleb even liked me that much. He was probably just craving attention. Who knows how long he's been here alone.

. . . .

The next day starts out normal, with Annabeth and I watching TV some more after our usual breakfast with everyone else, when a nurse enters the room. She looks between us both, then whispers, "Skylar?"

"That's me," I say. "What is it?" I grow anxious.

The nurse smiles warily at me. "You have a visitor."

Annabeth turns to me. "*What?*"

I swallow. Who would possibly want to visit me? "Who is it?" I ask, sitting up straighter in my bed, the covers falling to my waist.

"Come see," the nurse says.

"Good luck," Annabeth murmurs, a bit of jealousy caked over her voice.

I don't bother getting dressed up or anything, just follow the nurse slowly from the room, somewhat afraid although a strange satisfaction rises in the pit of my stomach. I can't tell if the satisfaction is from happiness or from the mystery of this unknown visitor.

The nurse quietly takes me into a small room. From what I can see before I enter, it's an office. I walk in and see her.

"Andria?" I gasp.

She turns. Her eyes are red as though she's been crying, and there are purple and blue circles beneath them from lack of sleep. Her hair is pretty, though, silky and smooth over her shoulders. I wonder if she's been using a new shampoo. Her freckles twinkle under the lights as she steadily smiles at me, her warm expression cautious. "Hey, Skylar," she says gently, taking me in from head to toe. "You look ... well."

I nod. She's wearing jeans, a blue and white striped blouse, and Chucks. Her style is *much* better than it was before, which is actually quite recently. I wonder why. And I think she's lost weight, too.

"I'll leave you two alone," the nurse says, backing out of the room and shutting the door.

"It's been... a long time, huh?" Andria says, managing a shy laugh, her voice echoing around the room as her brown eyes glitter.

"Yeah," I reply dimly, pressing my lips into a line. Her eyes fall to the floor. "Andria?" She looks up quickly. "Why are you here?"

She fakes a smile. "What? You're… you're my best friend—"

"No," I butt in flatly, closing my eyes. "I'm not. I was. But not anymore." When she doesn't say anything and the silence bites against my ears, my eyes peel open. Her eyes water as she stares into mine. "You're not my friend. You never were."

I can see her heart breaking through her eyes. I wonder if I looked as pathetic as her when she broke mine. "Sky…."

"*No*," I say, gritting my teeth. "Don't call me that." A tear falls down my face. I hadn't realized I was crying.

"I'm sorry," she breathes out, turning to face a wall. "I wanted to come sooner, but I was afraid."

"Afraid of what? Admitting to me that you were with my ex while he and I were dating? Admitting to me that the two of you planned it all out so I'd break up with him and you could have him all to yourself? Your little selfish self?" She tries to avoid my gaze, wiping her nose with a trembling finger. "You're afraid of admitting to me that you broke me, crushed me to get what you wanted." I laugh then. "No, not even admitting it to *me*, but to your *pathetic* self." She turns to me then, her mouth widened in utter defeat, her eyes swimming in guilt. "Thanks for coming to check on me, but sadly, you aren't my friend. I have to go back to my *actual* friend. But I hope you and Matt live a wonderful life together."

I turn and head to the door when I hear her call, "Stop, Skylar. Let me talk."

I quit walking but I don't know why. My feet won't move. For some reason I wish to hear her explanation. "Then talk," I say.

I hear her breathe in. "Matt is an idiot. He's the reason I came. He… he…." She swallows. "I broke up with him."

A warmth rises in my stomach then, and I gasp. But my anger stays put and I sigh. "Like that fixes anything."

"I want to start over," she cries. "I miss you. I didn't know that I did this to you."

"*What?*" I ask sharply, peering over my shoulder.

"I did this to you. Matt and I both did. We made you sick."

I laugh, turning back to face her. "You think *you* did this to me? See, you really are selfish, aren't you?" I shake my head. "Ridiculous."

"Why *are* you here, then?" she asks, furrowing her eyebrows.

"*Not* because of you," I snap. "You miss me? Well, guess what? I don't miss you one bit. What you did to me made me realize how much of a terrible, disgusting person you are!"

"Stop it!" she screams, her face reddening. "I get it, you're mad. I understand I did something awful to you. But I broke up with him for you. I want you, not him."

"Well, whoop-dee-doo," I growl. "Sorry, then, if that's the case. Because now you've lost both of us." I smile at her, my cheeks hot. "Have a good life." And then I leave, storming away from her.

When I reach my room, Annabeth asks who it was. I smile. "Nobody," I say, climbing back into bed. I grip the covers hard within my sweaty palms, the frustration rising inside forcing me to tremble.

. . . .

I'm excited to see Mrs. Carter the following day. I wake up bright and early to get dressed. I want to see how she's recovered, if she has.

Annabeth peers at me as I throw my hair into a ponytail in the bathroom, the light creating a line over my face. I'm still a bit upset from yesterday, but I'm not planning on telling Mrs. Carter. Why? I don't know why. I feel as though what happened was only between Andria and me.

I stare at myself in the mirror, realizing I've aged. I can see it in my face and I can feel it in my skin. Moments like this—like staring at yourself in the mirror—frighten me because I can clearly see that I'm growing up. I get all deep in thought then, pressing my fingers to the cold glass. *This is me.* I set a palm on my head and close my eyes. *All that's happened, and all there is in my life, is right here in my mind. How bizarre that is.*

"You okay, Sky?" Annabeth asks.

I open my eyes and quickly lower my hand as though it's a sin to wonder. "Great," I reply, looking at her in the mirror.

. . . .

"Skylar! How wonderful it is to see you!" Mrs. Carter exclaims as I enter the room. She stands and hugs me, holding me tight. I awkwardly press my hands on her back while I let her hold me until she decides to let go, looking me in the eye with a wide smile plastered across her face. "How *are* you?" she asks.

"Good," I say. "But shouldn't I be asking *you* that?"

She laughs and makes her way back to her seat while I do the same. It feels odd being here somehow, as though I don't belong anymore.

"I'm doing great," she says once she settles into her chair. "Thanks to you, of course. I left him, actually." She smiles. "I moved in with one of my friends who lives nearby, and I'll stay with her until the divorce papers are done and I get a place of my own. I've been thinking of getting a tiny house. I've always wanted one."

"Aren't you not supposed to tell me this stuff?" I ask her softly. For some reason, her unusually chatty self is unnerving.

She nods. "Yes, so don't tell, okay? But anyway, I finally feel as though my life is on track. It's a great feeling, huh?"

"It is," I say with a smile.

"You seem troubled by something," she tells me, observing carefully. "Are you all right?"

"Oh yes," I reply quickly. "I've just been thinking these past few days. It's nice to have time to think."

"It certainly is," Mrs. Carter agrees, nodding. "I'm glad you enjoyed your time off, as I definitely have. I figured the three quiet days would do you all good. What have you been thinking about?"

"How it seems so long ago that I went to that world," I say. "I don't feel like I was once somewhere else at all now."

"Interesting. It has been a long time, I agree. Actually, I was going to tell you… you return home in a week."

My insides tighten as I peer at her in confusion. "*What?*"

She smiles bitterly. "Obviously, you're much better. Your mother wants you to return home."

"But…," I start, very surprised my mother even thought about me. "why so soon? I don't think I'm ready, Susan. I still… I don't want to go." The thought of school… Andria, Matt, Mom… it makes my stomach churn.

"I know," she says. "And we can set up weekly counseling sessions until you're finally comfortable and feel at peace."

"You can't make me go," I snap.

She stares at me sadly. "I'm sorry. If I thought you needed more time here, I wouldn't let you go back home, but you are certainly better."

"But I haven't even finished explaining what happened!" I say. "And you still haven't diagnosed me and figured out what's wrong and—"

"Skylar," she hisses. "I'm sorry, but I am not your doctor, nor your mother." She breathes in deeply. "I don't want you to go, okay? I'm just doing what's best for you, which is going back home to your mother." When I don't say anything, she continues. "Now, about what happened. Would you like to revisit where we left off? I've been missing this."

twenty-two

A great roar startled us and we looked at each other with nervous glances. We had been awake inside the whale for hours, and that was the first moment anything bizarre—other than the fact that we were inside a whale, of course—had occurred. We were used to the weirdness, however; I could tell we were each prepared for whatever was about to happen.

The roar blared again and that time I stood, peering into the darkness. I wondered if there was another creature present. Had the whale swallowed something else? Tristan's steady breaths were the only other thing I was able to hear.

Then the ground began to shake; I fell and skinned my knees. I cried out as Tristan crawled to me.

"Skylar! Are you all right?"

Before I could speak, it suddenly began to flood. The water was swift, pouring in from somewhere unknown. Tristan and I screamed as we stood quickly, the water at our ankles. Then to our calves. Our knees. It wouldn't stop rising. Was the whale sinking? Had it died? With our recent luck, most likely.

Tristan and I drew close to one another. He grabbed my hand and squeezed, but I was too panicked to concentrate on him. I couldn't figure out where the water was coming from.

Soon enough, we found ourselves floating, the water sweeping us off our feet. It was at our shoulders, and we began rising with it. The water was ice cold and salty, burning against my numbing skin. I could feel the iced air bite my face, coming from the same hidden opening the water was pouring in from. My entire body shivered, my feet confused as where to step, my toes iced.

I heard the roar again, despite the loud noise from the rushing water. I turned to Tristan. "I think he's trying to talk to us!"

"What!" he hollered back, his hair wet and swept over his frightened eyes.

Another roar. "He wants us to relax!"

"*What?*"

"Go underwater!"

"You're insane!"

Roar.

"Let go of me and go underwater!"

"But—"

I swam down to the bottom, and after a few seconds, Tristan surprisingly followed me. I closed my eyes, the water rushing through the gaps between my fingers. I sank down... down... deep...

And then everything went blurry, hazy... and I no longer felt my skin.

. . . .

Tristan was shaking me intensely. All of a sudden, I coughed. He rolled me to my side as the salty ocean water poured from my blue lips. Being awake, I felt oddly cold, an unwelcome chill running up my spine. And coughing up the water was dreadful, the salt scratching my throat. When I thought I was done, more came after that. Tristan placed a careful hand on my back, which comforted me and forced me to relax.

Once I was finally finished, I lay back down on the cold, soft ground. I opened my eyes, the sunlight burning them furiously. I gritted my teeth as I looked to the blue, bright sky. "Are you okay?" Tristan asked, kneeling over me.

I nodded, swallowing to help soothe my itchy esophagus. But it didn't really help much.

"Okay, well let me just say…." He breathed in. "You are an *idiot!*"

Shocked, my eyes found his. They were wide and irritated as his forehead wrinkled and a frown found a comforting home on his lips.

My heartbeat picked up beneath my achy chest. "W-what?" I stuttered with a dry, hoarse voice, which led to me sitting up and coughing some more, that time without the water. My entire body was hot and sore, even in the cold.

"We almost *died* because of you!" Tristan cried out. I looked at him again. The anger plastered over his face made me stiffen. "If I would've gone underwater the same time as you, we would both be *dead!*"

"Wait," I heaved out. "What happened?"

He chuckled evilly. "You want to know what happened? We blew out of a whale's air hole and landed onto some snow."

I somehow managed a smile. "That may have possibly been the weirdest thing you've ever said."

He blinked at me, trying to remain furious, but the humor took the better of him and he smirked. "Not the *weirdest*, I bet."

I turned from him, staring out to the horizon. He was right; we definitely landed on snow. There was nothing but white nothingness for miles, besides the bit of ocean just a few yards behind us. The water was frozen over, however, too cold to swim in and too still to hear. The wind bit the tip of my nose harshly. "What now?" I asked quietly.

"You think *I* have a clue?" he snapped, his frustration returning. "I just saw you dead. I had to do CPR, or at least try to, for like ten minutes."

I turned to him then, my expression plain somehow. I saw the pain in his face, the fear lining his eyes as the recent memories returned. "I thought you were *dead*, Skylar. I was so afraid." My stomach plummeted as his eyes watered and his bottom lip quivered. I stared back at him, my eyes easily softening as I realized he saved my life.

"I died?" I asked.

"You didn't have a pulse," he said bluntly, turning away to look at the snow. "So, yeah."

I didn't say anything for a while, nor did he. The gentle winds were the only sounds my ears seemed to pick up. A wave of emotions washed over me and, in a way, refreshed me. I closed my eyes. "I forgive you."

"What?"

I opened my eyes to look at him softly. "I forgive you for slicing my thigh and running away."

He stared at me blankly for a moment, and then his gaze softened and a dim smile appeared on his face.

That's when my stomach roared. Had I not realized until then how starving I was? How parched? I swallowed, looking around for my bag, but it was gone. Had I left it in the whale? When was the last I had it? My palms grew sweaty.

"What's wrong?" Tristan asked, mildly concerned.

"I'm starving," I gasp. "Didn't you hear my stomach growl?"

He shook his head. "But yeah, I'm famished, too."

I peered around the snow. "I doubt there's anything to eat here."

"Then we better move fast," he said, beginning to stand. Then he cried out and collapsed onto the ground. I yelped his name as I kneeled over him. I had forgotten he had a wound, and even forgotten he was nearly dead. The sudden realization destroyed me silently, and a very sick feeling took over the pit of my stomach as I scanned over Tristan's awfully pale body.

"No," I said flatly. "We'll stay here until you're well. I don't care if I'm a bit hungry."

He looked up at me through squinted eyes. "I'm never going to get well, Skylar. I'm going to die."

"Shut up!" I screamed, gritting my teeth. "You're not going to—"

"Go, Skylar."

I blinked. "What?"

"Go find food. I'm going to die anyway. I'm just extra weight you have to carry."

I laughed bitterly. "Wait, are you *kidding*?"

He stared up at me with wet eyes and my face fell. "*No*," I said. "You're insane. *No*."

"Skylar," he croaked. "*Please*."

"No!" I cried out as a single tear fell down my cheek. "I don't care. I'm not leaving you."

He sighed, closing his eyes. "You hated me before."

"Well, now I don't."

"Why are you staying with me?" he breathed.

"The same reason you saved me just a few minutes ago," I mumbled, my throat clogged with deep melancholy. "I don't want you to die."

"And staying with me will somehow heal me?" he asked softly. He seemed very tired.

"No," I said. "I don't know… I want to stay with you."

"Then you're going to die."

"Then so be it," I said. "I probably will either way."

He tried to sit up, moaning. I made him lie back down, his head on my thighs as he breathed heavily and quickly. "I don't know why it's all hurting so bad," he whispered. "Maybe it's happening." I didn't reply. "Skylar, if I turn into one of those things, please—"

"*Shush*," I interrupted. "I don't want to talk about that. Not if it's happening. I want to talk about other stuff."

"Okay. It hurts to talk."

I swallowed, my eyes watering. I didn't know what to do. It seemed as though there was nothing more I could do. But then, surprisingly, I began to sing "Stand By Me," a song Dad used to sing to me when I was upset

"60s, huh?" he croaked out, interrupting my singing.

"Shh," I said, my voice oddly cracked because of the returning of my regular voice. "Don't talk. But yes, I love 60s."

"You have a beautiful voice," he murmured, his voice slurred. "So… beautiful."

I looked down at his limp body and found myself blushing. "My dad loved 60s. He loved my voice, too." I glanced up and scanned my eyes over the distant horizon. "Before he left, he'd play 60s music all the time. He and my mom would dance and dance all night while I was supposed to be asleep. I'd peer around the corner, just watching them laugh. I took those moments for granted. I haven't seen my mother smile, *truly* smile, since."

I swallowed, remembering the sensations. Remembering my father and my mother, how they were so happy together. I looked back down at Tristan again. "Tristan?"

"Hmm?" he purred.

I began to play with his hair, stroking it softly with my clammy fingers. "One day, maybe we could dance together." He stirs a bit but doesn't reply. I close my eyes and relax. My stomach roars again, but I am not hungry anymore.

. . . .

I began thinking deeply of myself then. Who I was at that moment and how I've changed since I ventured there in my apparent sleep. As I sat there upon the snow, Tristan lying nearly lifeless in my lap, a great anxiety blanketed me, forcing me to rethink everything that had happened. I tried to figure out how I appeared back home. Was I in a coma? In the hospital? Were Mom and Dad there, watching over me and holding hands, hoping my eyes would suddenly peel open, or was I completely alone in the room? Or had I entirely disappeared? I wondered if I had gone missing in New York City, and if there were pictures of me taped to streetlights. I even got so deep into my head that I wondered if my life on Earth had even existed, and if *it* was all just an alternate reality, rather than this one.

I glanced down at Tristan, my lips frosted over in ice, my eyelashes rock solid, and my skin pure white. I could no longer move my hands or feet; I was so terribly weak. What do you do in that situation? What are you supposed to do? I didn't know because I was alone and afraid. I wanted to go home, yet at the same time I didn't, for despite the unwelcoming emptiness I felt within, being there with Tristan gave me a satisfying warmth that seemed to keep me awake just a little bit longer. But then again, such a feeling couldn't keep me alive. My surroundings blurred and the brightness of the sun dimmed. And then I felt nothing.

Until several warm hands lifted me from the snow, that is. I tried to speak, but no words came. I couldn't even create sounds, so I decided to relax as they carried me the rest of the way to wherever we were going, hoping Tristan was beside me or at least behind me, going to the same place I was, whether that be another realm or not.

twenty-three

Homecoming was amazing in that green dress I bought, the one I apparently looked and felt so good in. I went with Matt, Andria, and one of Andria's other friends so she wouldn't be third-wheeling. Andria wore a red dress, tight with a tutu-like end. She looked stunning, with light red eye shadow and just a bit of mascara; that's all she needed.

Matt wore a tuxedo with an emerald green tie to match my dress. His black hair was nicely slicked back and he looked *amazing*.

Once we arrived, Andria and her other friend— Laura, I think—ventured off to get food while Matt and I began dancing. It was a fast song, and I was twirling and he was laughing. And after three more quick songs, a slow one came on. Matt gave me a look, grinning, and gently set his palm on my hip, pulling me closer to him. I wrapped my arms around his neck and laid my head on his shoulder, closing my eyes and feeling his warm breath on my ear. "You look gorgeous tonight," he whispered. "I love you." My stomach filled with butterflies.

That was the last night we "hung out." After, he began treating me like crap. And ever since, I've been wondering if what he whispered in my ear as we were dancing had been for me, or for someone else.

. . . .

"So when were you ever going to tell me what happened with you and your ex-best-friend?" Annabeth asks me that night on our way back from dinner.

I look at her, raising an eyebrow. "I don't... I'm confused."

She laughs. "You think I wouldn't figure it out? It was pretty obvious." She sighs. "You don't tell me anything. Caleb. Your ex-best-friend. Stop holding it in and tell me!" She laughs again. "It gets boring here without drama!"

I sigh as we approach the door to our room. "Nothing happened. She said hi and left." I open the door and walk in, flopping on my bed.

Annabeth shuts the door behind her and raises an eyebrow to me. "Mmhmm," she purrs.

"No, really," I say, sitting cross-legged. I stare at a nearby wall. "I mean, she apologized, too. But like that changes anything."

"Why don't you give her a chance?" she asks, strolling to her bed and lying down, staring at the ceiling. "She obviously cares about you or she wouldn't have shown up."

"But what she did to me was awful!" I scream. She glances at me. "She did dump my ex, though."

"See?" she says, smiling. "Don't end your friendship over some guy."

"*Annabeth!*" I yell, gritting my teeth. "Did I not tell you what she did? She hurt me *so* bad."

"But she didn't do it intentionally. She was in love." I swallow as Annabeth sits up on the bed, facing me with soft eyes. "I think you've forgotten that we're all still clumsy children just wanting someone to love and to love us back."

I blink at her. "But…." I look at the floor.

"Just put yourself in her shoes. She ended it with someone she loved so you could understand she meant no harm. She and your ex worked out a lot better than you and him, which is hard to realize. Some people just fit better together than others. Trust me, I had to learn the hard way, too." I gaze up at her. She presses her lips into a line. "Just… when you get back home, whenever that may be, give her a chance."

"Next week," I say quickly.

She squints then, leaning forward. "*What?*"

"I know. Mom wants me back home."

She shakes her head. "But you've barely even been here that long."

I nod, turning away.

"You can't leave me," Annabeth whimpers. I look back up at her, notice her eyes are wet. "You're the only true friend I've ever had."

I bite my bottom lip. "But don't you live in New York, too? We can visit."

She shakes her head. "I'm moving."

"Where?"

"I don't know."

"What do you mean, 'you don't know'?"

"My dad went to jail," she tells me softly. "And my mom wants nothing to do with me, remember? The doctors here are trying to find foster families and orphanages who will take a sick seventeen-year-old who is nearly eighteen. But they haven't had much luck."

I just stare at her. "I'm sorry."

"Don't be. I'll be okay." She smiles weakly.

"Wait," I say quickly, standing from the bed and pacing the room. "You can live with me!"

"Huh?"

I smile, looking her straight in the eye. "You can live with me! We can get a job together and save up for an apartment for ourselves! Yes! And until then, you can go to school with me and we can have sessions together, and we can just work after school and on weekends. It'll be great! Yes! It'll be—"

"Skylar," Annabeth interrupts, standing up and walking over to me. She grips my shoulders hard. "Would your mother even allow that?"

"Knowing her," I say, "she wouldn't mind at all."

Annabeth swallows.

"I mean, we can try, right? It doesn't hurt to try!"

Annabeth starts crying then, and I stare at her in concern. "What's wrong?" I ask.

"Nothing," she says, a smile appearing beneath her tears. "I've just never had someone like you in my life who cares for me this much. I've had just an awful life."

"It's life. Crap happens. But good stuff happens, too."

She nods. "I never thought I'd find someone like you *here*, though."

"Welcome to the land of the freaks. *Anything* can happen here."

. . . .

I go to the counseling session knowing it will be my last one explaining the happening. It was nearly over, which made it all just seem so pointless. It took barely any time to tell the story, when in reality the experience lasted a lifetime.

I sit in my usual spot, my lips twisted and my thoughts blank.

"Skylar?" Mrs. Carter asks, confusion in her eyes.

twenty-four

I awoke in a cage on a hard, cold floor in a dark room. I peeled open my eyes, coughing out dust, my lips still frozen from being outside in the snow, my body weak from lack of food. My vision was blurry, but I could clearly see the shadows of the bars of the cage before me. And my senses were strong enough to smell the sweet scent of fresh bread. I quickly scrambled about the cage on hands and knees trying to scout it out. When I at last ran into the plate, piled with the bread I smelled as well as the same pink fruit I had from the forest, I ate most of it in less than a minute. The food filled my body with the taste of life, but also scratched my throat. I located a glass of cold water and chugged it to the very last drop. Wiping my mouth with the back of my hand, I sat back down on the cold floor, my vision clear at last.

I scanned the darkened room as I continued to eat the remaining fruit and bread. The cage was in the center, the bars reaching the ceiling and too close together for me to crawl through. I wondered who put me in that jail cell, but at the same time fed me and gave me some water. And I also wondered where the heck Tristan was.

I noticed then that I was dressed in fresh, yet unusual clothing. They were Egyptian styled, I think, with a light blue, bra-type top lined with gold and soft, light blue pants to match with a gold belt and trim down the sides. They were small at the waist but large and roomy down the legs, growing tight again at my calves. And my hair was still up in a bun, but neat and tied with a large piece of blue cloth. A single strand fell over my eyes.

I ran my fingers over the soft cloth. The fabric was beautiful, and I couldn't understand why someone would waste it on a prisoner like me. At least I thought I was a prisoner.

A young girl then suddenly entered the room from a once-hidden door that gently slid open, revealing a mysterious light that poured into the room like water. She was beautiful, with silky, cocoa brown hair, and atop her small head sat a lovely golden clip. She wore an outfit similar to mine, only with more gold jewelry—rings on every finger and a chain that attached her top to her pants—and hers was in white rather than the light blue of mine. She smiled at me as she made her way to the cage.

"Don't sit on floor," she said in an accent I did not recognize, her face falling once she approached me. "You'll get dirty."

I cautiously stood. It was strange to see another person besides Tristan. She seemed so real, so close to me. And she was much taller than I, with tan skin, even tanner than Zack Corley's. It appeared as smooth as the creamer my mom would pour into her coffee every morning. And her brown eyes twinkled. They were the kind of brown that didn't blend into her pupils; they stood out like vibrant jewels.

"I see you found food," she purred. "And water. Feel better?"

I nodded, pursing my lips.

"Good. Then you are ready."

"For what?" I asked softly.

"The battle."

"The battle?"

She nodded, grinning. "We do it with all new guests. A fun battle."

"I've never heard of a *fun* battle," I mumbled.

She smiled with perfect white teeth that glowed. "This battle is fun."

She began unlocking the cage and I started biting my fingernails, either out of anxiety or fear. "Where is Tristan?"

"Who?" she asked as she fumbled with the key and the lock. "*Oh* yes. The handsome boy who with you? You will see handsome boy soon."

"You think he's handsome?"

"Very." She laughed, the lock clicking within her palms and the door creaking open. "But do not tell, for it is forbidden."

I lowered my fingers from my chapped lips as I stared at her curiously. "It's forbidden to find other people handsome? That's strange."

She shook her head. "No. It is forbidden to love."

"What?"

"If you see a handsome man, you will love him eventually. That's where it begins, with attraction. So must be careful."

"Why is love forbidden?"

Her eyes grew hard. "Love equal heartbreak."

"Not always. Not with the right person."

"Even so," she said, "people die. Heartbreak."

"But—"

"There is no love here," she snapped, gritting her teeth. But then her face softened and she sighed. "But your handsome boy is very handsome. Please, do not tell."

"I won't," I told her.

She smiled. "Thank you. Now, follow me." She turned and exited the room through the same door. As directed, I followed.

The hallway was as dark and depressing as the room. There were branches lit with fire along the walls, putting a light shadow across the girl's back.

"Where are we going?" I asked her.

"Battlegrounds," she replied without hesitation.

"What happens if I lose?"

"You die."

I stopped. "Wait, *what?*"

She turned back to look at me, an eyebrow raised in confusion. "What is the problem?"

"I'm not going to fight to the death!" My heart was pounding in my chest.

"It'll be okay," she purred. "I do it once. Not hard."

I shook my head. "I'm not going."

"If you don't go, I kill you now." She pulled a shimmering dagger from a pocket in her silky pants.

I swallowed, looking at it.

"Sorry. I just follow orders. Now, come."

I looked to my feet and continued walking. I had been through so much already; I supposed this was not much of a surprise. I wondered who I was prepared to fight. If Tristan would be watching.

We soon arrived at two giant doors. She turned to me. "You will get a weapon you like as soon as you walk out the doors. King will explain the rest. Good luck, Skylar."

I would've asked how she knew my name but that wasn't my top priority at the moment. I nodded at her and pulled a door open. A bright flash of light stunned me, nearly pushing me over, and hot, dry air filled my lungs with an unsettling feeling. I squinted as I stepped out, my bare feet pressing against soft, hot sand that poured up through the gaps between my toes.

I blinked several times as my eyes adjusted to the arena setup. I felt as though I was in Rome, with the stands set up high above the oval of sand. It was huge, probably the length of two Olympic swimming pools. The crowd roared as I walked forward carefully. Everything was covered with a stone roof besides the oval of sand, which sat directly under the sun and seemed to glow by its radiance.

A man was suddenly beside me, his skin dark and rough like leather, hair light brown and shaggy with natural highlights. He was shirtless, wearing nothing but the same silky pants as me and the girl, but in brown and with less gold. He nodded, a way to greet me I figured, and pointed to a row of weapons on a stone wall. "Choose," he told me.

I strolled over to the wall, scanning the several choices. There were daggers, swords, maces, axes, and even ropes and staves. I picked up a brilliant sword, made of pure silver with an orangey-pink handle, the face of a lion in the center of the blade. It was huge and felt strange in my hand. Luckily, the blade was thin enough for me to carry with ease.

I continued walking through the sand, surprisingly not as terrified as I thought I'd be. Perhaps all the strange occurrences here made everything feel more and more like a dream.

"Welcome, Skylar!" cried the king from the stands. He wore gorgeous white and gold armor, a glinting crown atop his head. His skin was as dark as everyone else's, but he was much bigger than the rest. "I see you have picked the Sword of Leon. A popular choice. Now entering from the opposite side, your opponent!" The crowd cheered again.

My eyes found the doors opposite mine, exactly like the ones I had just entered through. They opened slowly, and out stepped a man. His head was bowed and he was also shirtless, wearing the same outfit as the man who pointed me to the weapons, except his pants were the same light blue as mine. He walked to the wall of weapons and chose a smaller sword than the one I grasped so tightly, then continued walking toward me. He wasn't as dark as the other men.

"Welcome, Tristan!" the king called out. "I see you've chosen the Silverglint. Excellent choice. Meet your opponent, Skylar! Oh, but wait! I'm afraid you already have! So now, you will meet once again... for the last time!"

The crowd erupted in laughter as my jaw dropped. Tristan eyed me, his expression sad. He stood only about ten yards from me and I could sense his withdrawal. He no longer had a gash on his chest. I supposed they had healed him.

But I was about to fight to the death against Tristan. I knew, as did he, that one would have to fall. How was I so oblivious before that I did not predict this?

I bit my bottom lip and closed my eyes, feeling Tristan's strong stare on me.

"The winner will stay to thrive with the rest of us! And the loser.... Well, let's just say don't be the loser! And let the fight *begin*!"

The crowd roared one last time before they hushed and watched us patiently. I opened my eyes as Tristan and I began slowly stepping toward one another,

our weapons held loosely in our sweaty hands. "Hey," I
said once I was close enough for him to hear.

"I'm not gonna kill you," he spat. Anger drowned
his eyes, and his face looked strangely older than before.
But he was still just as stunning, and him being shirtless
gave me butterflies. But the thought of killing him
flooded my mind. "I won't even fight you. I can't."

"You think *I* can?" I whispered.

He turned to face the king. "We will not fight in
your stupid battle!" he shouted with rage.

"Is that so?" the king replied, annoyed. I was
surprised he could hear Tristan. "Well, then I suppose we
will have to just kill you *both*. Release the beasts!"

A loud roar erupted then, and Tristan and I each
turned our gazes toward a large gate being lifted upwards
by a hefty, rusted metal chain. Out crawled a humongous
scorpion. Besides that, a snake -- just as giant -- slithered
out, and last came a coyote the size of a large wolf. They
all howled at the sky as the crowd clapped and whistled
with excitement.

Tristan and I exchanged glances and I found
myself laughing. He grinned back. "I'll admit," he told
me, "you look *stunning* in that outfit."

"Same to you," I replied, blushing. "Now let's do
this." I began walking toward the beasts, raising my sword
in the air. I think I was so put out by everything that I
began to go with it. Tristan was at my side, his sword just
as high, the tip of the blade kissing the cloudless sky.

The beasts began racing toward us. "I have an idea," I said. "I'll get the coyote. You try to get the scorpion and snake away."

"What?" he asked, his voice cracked in fear. "Why do *I* have to get two?"

"Trust me," I laughed. "Just distract them for a bit."

I began running toward the wall at my side, close to the coyote. It halted to stare at me curiously as Tristan ran between the scorpion and snake swiftly enough to gain their attention. The coyote then chased me into a corner and I turned, breathing heavily as I faced her snarl. She lashed out at me but I dodged it. And then I relaxed, closed my eyes. *I don't wish to hurt you,* I thought deeply. *Please, help us. We don't belong here and you know it.*

When I opened my eyes, the coyote looked at me, her head tilted to one side. I smiled and ran away, the coyote suddenly at my side. I had no clue how that worked, to be honest; I just assumed all the beings were connected and ran with it. Lucky me.

The coyote and I raced to where Tristan stood struggling as he sped quickly from the other two beasts. "Go to the scorpion!" I shouted to the coyote, and to my surprise she did as told, leaping onto the bug and sinking her canine teeth into its back. The scorpion roared, trying to shake off its attacker.

"The hell?" Tristan screamed at me. "What did you do?"

"Not important!" I yelled back. "Now follow me!"

We ran as the snake slithered behind us, hissing furiously. I hadn't thought as far as how to kill the snake, so until then we just sprinted around the arena, the sand spraying us all over.

Hiss... hiss... hiss....

As I ran, I began thinking of the word hiss, which led to me thinking of the word kiss. And of course, I thought about true love's kiss. My eyes widened as I thought... harder.... Could it be...?

"Skylar!" Tristan screamed. "We have to attack it!"

We stopped running. The snake caught up to us and I just peered at it.

Hiss.

"You distract it!" he bellowed. "I'll go around back."

But the snake did not attack me. Instead, I felt as though it were telling me something. I looked closely. Was it nodding?

Hisssssss.

"I don't want to hurt you," I whispered.

I know.

And the snake's eyes rolled back and it fell onto the sand. I looked up and saw Tristan's blade in the spine of the large reptile. He smiled, but I was not happy.

I turned to the scorpion and watched as it struck the coyote once... twice... and the coyote fell from its back, lifeless. My stomach fell as I ran to Tristan.

"Kiss me," I said, panicked.

"What?" He lifted an eyebrow, sweat forming on his forehead.

"Kiss me."

He looked behind me. "The scorpion is coming. We have to—"

"We can't kill it," I say. "And even if we do, everyone else will kill us, or we'll have to kill each other, and—"

"Skylar! We have to hurry!"

I grabbed his shoulders and his green eyes once again found mine, but they were anxious. "The door," I said. "What if it isn't a literal door? What if the way out is a *metaphor* to an actual door?"

"What?" His voice was labored from his exertion.

"It's a test, remember? You said it yourself, a test we have to take to prove we don't belong here." I looked at him deeply, trying to figure out if he understood, but he still seemed confused so I went on. "Love is forbidden here. In this place, in this world. There is no love allowed. They don't believe in such a thing. But you and I... I...." I swallowed. "The door is us, Tristan. We are the door."

He grew interested then, licking his lips.

"You have to kiss me. We have to try." I stared into his eyes earnestly.

"It's not time yet," he told me. "We can't leave now... I'm not ready to leave you.

"We have no choice."

He stared at me sadly. "What if it *is* all just a dream?"

"It's not. And I know it's not because—"

And that's when I felt the scorpion strike me. Well, I actually *didn't* feel it, but I knew it happened. You just kind of know at a moment like that.

"Skylar!"

I couldn't feel anything besides a strange pain in my upper chest as I stumbled to the ground, Tristan gripping my forearms tautly. He knelt beside me, pressing a hand to my head.

I looked at him, saw his wariness.

"I'm so sorry," he gasped, not being able to take in what just happened. "It should have been me. Gosh, why couldn't it have been *me*? I'm so sorry. Please, don't go. I'm not ready. I can't—"

"Shhhh," I whispered. "I'm not... gone... yet."

He looked into my eyes intensely. "Whatever happens, Skylar," he cried softly, trying to quickly find the words to say, "I will find you again. Whether it be back home in New York City the next day when—or if—we both wake up, or six years from now, or even in the afterlife... I will find you. Skylar, I... I love you."

Despite not being able to feel anything, a sudden warmth spread throughout my body and I found myself smiling through what I assumed was tears. "I... love... you... Tristan..." I managed to croak out.

"Wait for me, okay? Wait for me and I will find you. I promise." He swallowed. "Good-bye, Skylar."

I could no longer make out his face but I saw his figure lean down. Then, ever so gently, I felt his lips press against mine, soft and hesitant at first, but then powerful. He grasped my face within his warm palms, kissing me so sweetly and beautifully. All of these feelings surrounded me, filled my insides, and a wild breeze blew around us. But then my body lightened, and his lips fell from mine. I wanted to cry out to him, tell him not to leave, but by then it was too late. I was gone, and so was he.

Good-bye, Tristan.

twenty-five

I woke up in my bed. *My* bed. Back home. As though nothing had ever happened.

It was about five thirty in the morning. I hadn't exactly realized what had just occurred in my apparent sleep, but hazy feelings drowned out my thoughts. I slipped from the bed and strolled uneasily to the kitchen. My eyes were wide, glazed over. I was terribly thirsty.

I fetched a cup from the kitchen and filled it halfway with tap water, but before I drank it, I dropped it.

Mom exited her room. "What the hell are you doing up this early? Go back to bed." I just stared at her. She squinted at me. "Go to bed, Sky, or I'll make you go."

The thoughts began appearing then. Waking up alone… an abandoned city… giant cats….

"Skylar!"

"It wasn't a dream," I say.

"What? Clean this mess up right now! Why'd you spill water everywhere? Clean it up and go back to bed. *Now.*"

Then suddenly… *Tristan.* I screamed.

"Skylar Vail! Stop it!"

But I wouldn't stop. I screamed as loud as I possibly could until my throat burned. Tears poured from my eyes as I began scrambling about the house. "Where is he? Where is Tristan?"

Mom watched me from the kitchen. I think she was scared.

"It wasn't a dream.... It wasn't a dream.... Where *is* he? No! *No*! I *love* him! Where is he? I want him back!"

I was wheezing and bawling, pressing my hands to my head and squeezing my eyes closed so hard I could see stars beneath my eyelids. I tried to get the images out of my head but they wouldn't move. The memories screamed to me. I screamed harder to overpower their voices.

"You just had a bad dream," Mom whispered cautiously.

"It wasn't a dream!" I snapped at her, opening my eyes and lowering my hands.

And then I grabbed a knife.

"Skylar... put that down."

"No!" I screamed. "It wasn't a dream!" I stared at the knife. "I want to go back. I need to go back. I need to die to go back. I want to die, Mom." I looked back up at her, saw she was crying.

"I love him."

And that is the last I remember of that night.

twenty-six

Dear Dad,

Hey. I know it's been a while. I've tried to call, but you just don't answer. Maybe a letter will be better.

Anyway, I don't know if Mom told you or not, but I haven't been well these past few weeks. I'm better now, but I had a bad dream a while ago and it sort of made me go crazy. I used to think it wasn't a dream, actually.

Currently I'm at a hospital. I leave in two days, though. Tomorrow is my last real day here, and I'm actually sort of sad. Who knew a hospital would be so much fun? Mom actually asked for me to go home, and that makes me really happy, to be honest. I didn't think Mom wanted me anymore. But maybe she does. Maybe things will be different when I get home. One can only hope.

I don't think you care about any of this, but Mrs. Carter (she lets me call her Susan), my counselor, told me the cause of the dream was because of abandonment. Not saying it's your fault, but I am saying you're one of the causes. You, as well as Mom, Andria, and Matt. I basically dreamt that I was alone besides a guy named Tristan, and he and I ventured through this weird world together. I was diagnosed with depression, so I now have to take pills until I'm better, and I'll have to talk to Mrs. Carter until I'm no longer depressed.

You've missed a lot of my life. I still wonder why you left. Mom is still sad over you. And I'll admit that so am I. I looked up to you a lot when I was little, for basically everything. Before Andria (who no longer is my friend), you were my best friend. I hope you come back one day because right now my life's pretty boring.

I have to go back home to Mom and I'm kind of afraid. I'm also afraid to see Andria and Matt in school. But I think, after talking to Annabeth, that I'll try to forgive Andria. I think it'd be good for me to forgive her, let the pain go. And I really hope Mom lets Annabeth live with us. Annabeth is my new best friend.

Also, my new favorite color is emerald green. And my favorite animal is a whale. Just in case you ever want to buy me a birthday present one year.

I probably won't actually give you this letter. Mrs. Carter told me to write one to let my last bit of emotions out. She wanted me to forgive you, too, so I guess I forgive you.

I hope you have a good life with your new wife and new family. I love you, Dad.

I guess that's all I have left to say to you.

Your loving daughter,

Skylar Vail

twenty-seven

"It is sad to say that this is Skylar's last day of group counseling," Mrs. Carter tells us once we're all seated. She's pouting. "We'll just have to make this group session the best one there is!"

"Agreed," Annabeth says, nudging me with her elbow.

"Of course," Caleb grumbles, letting out a rough sigh.

"But first," Mrs. Carter says, "we have somebody new who is going to be joining us. He's a bit shy, so let's make sure we're all welcoming, okay?"

"Perfect timing," I laugh.

The door to the office slowly opens and there stands Dr. Richards with a large smile on his face. "Hello, everyone."

Then, from behind him, he walks in with his dark brown hair and emerald green eyes. He stops once he sees me, his eyes wide and his lips slightly parted. For just a moment, the world stops turning and it is just him and me, our racing hearts and quick breaths. A smile melts onto his lips once he realizes it's no longer a dream.

But then again, perhaps it still is. And I wonder to myself then. I suppose I will never quite know if this world we live in is a true reality or an alternate one. If all we have ever thought was real—all the little things like relationship troubles, friend drama, weird parent issues, and just crappy things in general—if those things are even real at all. Perhaps, if you truly believe, our dreams are more than just dreams. Our dreams make us. Our dreams *are* our reality.

"Welcome, Tristan," Mrs. Carter says. "Please, have a seat."

But then again, who really knows for sure?

247 | F o r s a k e n

acknowledgements

Writing a novel as a high-school student certainly isn't easy, but to me, being young wasn't an excuse. I spent long days and nights crafting my first published work, rather than doing typical teenage girl things ... but I couldn't have done any of this without my amazing supporters.

First off, thank you to Rocky Callen, a book coach, who first introduced me to my cover designer, Najla Qamber, and my editors from Hot Tree Editing (also, a *huge* thank you to these two!). I've always wanted to self-publish – I love doing things on my own, I suppose – and Rocky gave me the support I needed to continue my journey.

Also, a big thank you to my family and friends who read Forsaken during its rough, under-developed form, and who still, to this day, help me with Forsaken's journey, as well as other creations.

about me

You may know me, actually. I'm not too difficult to recognize. I'm not some superstar or anyone popular, I'm just me!

I am the sixteen-year old brunette in the back of the classroom with her nose in a book and her thoughts in another world; my imagination always seems to force me to drift away from reality, which causes my writing to differ from others. And I *love* cats, nature, swimming and every one of my *amazing* friends and family members!

I was born and raised in Texas. Once I graduate high school (2018), I will hopefully become a counselor, helping teenagers who have gone through trauma, and I will write several more books along the way. My goal is to leave a beautiful impression on the world.

Thank you for reading my first novel! Every one of you has impacted me greatly! I hope you all enjoyed reading this book as much as I did writing it!

And I will for sure miss you, Skylar Vail. Farewell for now, my friend.

- Probably Writing,
Brittney

Anything is possible,
if only you believe it is!

CONTACT ME

instagram - @brittneykristinabooks

facebook - www.facebook.com/BrittneyKx

www.BrittneyKristinaBooks.com

CPSIA information can be obtained
at www.ICGtesting.com
Printed in the USA
BVOW03s1854170717
489519BV00001B/5/P